STARDUST

Other Avon Camelot Books by
Alane Ferguson

CRICKET AND THE CRACKERBOX KID
THE PRACTICAL JOKE WAR

Avon Flare Books

OVERKILL
SHOW ME THE EVIDENCE

ALANE FERGUSON says, "I've always loved the magic of reading because some characters are as real to me as people I know.

"Now when kids write to me about Cricket or Dominic or other friends they've met in my books, it's the greatest thrill."

Alane Ferguson lives in Sandy, Utah, with her husband, Ron, and their three children, Kristin, Danny, and Kathy.

STARDUST

ALANE FERGUSON

AN AVON  CAMELOT BOOK

AVON BOOKS
A division of
The Hearst Corporation
1350 Avenue of the Americas
New York, New York 10019

Copyright © 1993 by Alane Ferguson
Published by arrangement with Bradbury Press
Library of Congress Catalog Card Number: 92-33011
ISBN: 0-380-72321-2
RL: 4.9

First Avon Camelot Printing: January 1995

CAMELOT TRADEMARK REG. U.S. PAT. OFF. AND IN OTHER COUNTRIES, MARCA REGISTRADA, HECHO EN U.S.A.

Printed in the U.S.A.

OPM 10 9 8 7 6 5 4 3 2

To Maureen Hayes
whose light has touched us all

"Look, Mom, it's Samantha Love! I want to get her autograph! Do you have a pen? Hurry, Mom, she's getting away! Stop, Samantha! I'm your hugest fan!''

Haley felt her stomach squeeze as she heard the shouting behind her. She had hoped her large, cat's-eye sunglasses and Dodgers baseball cap would keep the pesky fans away, but they always seemed to recognize her. And she wasn't in the mood to be pawed over. Not now.

Ducking behind a large palm tree, Haley stole a glance in the direction of the voices. A pudgy boy with pasty white skin pulled his mother along by the hand.

''Wait a minute, Tyson, I'm trying to find a pen and my purse is a mess! Are you positive that was Samantha Love?''

''For sure it's her. Come on, Mom, she went behind that tree! This is the first time I've ever met a real live star, and if you don't hurry up, I'm gonna lose her! Samantha! Samantha Love!''

Darn—Haley thought—she'd been caught! It was no

use trying to get away, so she crossed her arms, leaned against the rough bark of the palm tree, and waited. Seconds later, the boy rounded the tree and skidded to a stop. Even though his body stood still, it seemed as though his eyes kept right on going. They practically popped out of his face. His mouth moved, but no words came out. Finally, he managed to squeak, "Wow!"

"Oh, my goodness, it *is* you! It's Samantha Love!" the mother puffed as she ran into the back of her son. Tyson made an "oomph" sound. Haley thought he looked sweaty.

"I can't believe it! You look older than you look on television! Oh, you are so cute!" the mother chattered. "We watch you every Thursday night, and we think your show is the greatest. Don't we, Tyson? If our family has a little squabble, we stop and say, 'Let's love like the Love Family.' Then just like that!"—she snapped her fingers—"we all hug each other and smile. Don't we, Tyson? Say something, Tyson."

"Wow."

The mother handed Haley the back of an old shopping list and a sticky pen. Looking almost shy, she asked, "Could you—would you sign this for me and Tyson? Just write, 'To my best friends Lily and Tyson'—that's T-Y-S-O-N—'oodles of kisses from Samantha Love.' "

Haley grabbed the paper and scribbled "Haley Loring" and handed it back.

"Ever since you did those Air Soft Diaper commercials when you were just a wee little baby, Tyson would look at the TV and say, 'I wuv her.' Isn't that precious? 'I wuv her.' "

"MOTHER!" Tyson wailed. Haley didn't know a

human being could get that red. He almost disappeared into his blush.

"Well, you did!" His mother beamed. She glanced down at the autograph. Her smiled faded. "Wait a minute—this isn't right."

"It's my name!" Haley snapped. "I mean—puleeze—I am not Samantha Love! I'm Haley Loring, an actress who plays Samantha Love."

"But—"

"When I sign autographs, I sign MY name, okay!"

Tyson looked as if he wanted to sink into the ground. His mother's head bobbed up and down in a vigorous nod. "Of course we understand. Thank you, Haley, for your autograph. Let's go, Tyson."

Haley felt a pang of guilt shoot through her like a hot arrow. Even though her whole world had just fallen apart, there was no reason to take it out on her fans. It wasn't fair.

"Wait!" Haley cried. "Let me have that paper again."

She quickly wrote, "Oodles of kisses from Samantha Love" and then drew little hearts all around. When she gave it back, Tyson grinned so big that Haley could see his back teeth. "If you only knew how much we love you," his mother said. They waved at her as they walked away. Haley waved back.

If you only knew that everything in my life is all over, Haley whispered to herself. If you only knew.

Haley opened the sliding glass door and stepped onto their redwood deck. Large terra-cotta pots held miniature palm trees. Pink and red roses bloomed from redwood boxes, and the fragrance of the blossoms mingled with the smell of the sea. Kicking off her sneakers, Haley stepped into the cool sand and felt it slip between her toes. She looked down at her long, slender feet. Too long. Just like the rest of her body. She'd grown. Shot up from the darling, button-nosed little girl that she'd once been. Now she was gawky. Hadn't her agent, Sheena Byrd, said that just last week? Haley cringed at the memory of it.

"I'm afraid I've got some bad news for you," Sheena had told them, touching her long polished fingernails together at the tips. "I just got the call. The 'Family Love' ratings dropped again; the studio decided to . . . well, rework the show. Your character, Samantha Love, is going off to a boarding school in Europe. You're being written off the show, Haley. I'm sorry."

Leaning forward, Haley's dad asked, "Can they do

that? Can they just get rid of her without any warning?''

"The studio can do anything it wants. It's in Haley's contract, if you'd like to check. I've got it right here. And, Haley, darling, don't bite your nails. You've still got your farewell episode to shoot. We mustn't have chewed-up fingers for the cameras, must we?''

With a smack, Haley's hand landed in her lap.

"Now, Sheena," her father began. "We've been through a lot together. I know how much power you have here in Hollywood. Can't you call the big guns at the studio, or the writers on 'Family Love,' or somebody, and get Haley back on the show?''

Picking up an onyx pen, Sheena rolled it between her palms. Her red nails looked like claws.

"It's out of my hands, Ben," she said. "The studio sent tapes of 'Family Love' to random people across the United States. They wanted to try and find out what was going wrong with the show. Unfortunately, the study showed that people just don't respond well to the Samantha character anymore.''

Almost choking, her mother asked, "Why?''

"A couple of reasons," Sheena declared. "First, Samantha's lines were funny when they were said by a little girl. But she's grown quite a lot this past year. The lines aren't funny when they're said by a preteen. In fact, a lot of the adults saw Samantha as a real smart-mouth, and didn't want their children to watch her.''

"But that's the writers' fault!" her father exploded. "Haley just reads the lines that are handed to her! How can you dump Haley when she was just following directions? How—''

Her father kept talking, but Haley didn't hear. She

5

couldn't make sense of the words that flew around her, couldn't string them together to make a sentence that she could understand. It was hard to think. Her brain felt frozen. All except one word that went through her mind over and over again. Dumped. She was being dumped, written off. "Family Love" didn't want her anymore. She was too big. Too tall. Too something. It was over. As Sheena's and her parents' words filled the room, Haley commanded her mind to think of something else. Anything else. Color. Everything in Sheena's office was black, white, or red. Even Sheena. Her ebony hair was pulled back in a sleek bun, and her skin was as white as bleached flour. Perfect ruby-red lips had been carefully painted on. When she smiled, her teeth looked gleaming white. Black, white, and red. As Sheena handed her father some papers, Haley had made a mental list of everything that fit the pattern: black couch, red chairs, white walls. Black desk, red phone, white lamp. Black sculpture, red vase, white orchids.

"Haley, darling, pay attention," Sheena said. "This is about you."

Her mother crossed her arms and clutched her elbows. Haley could tell she was almost crying. "Okay. If we have to accept it, we have to accept it. What does all this mean to Haley's career? Do you have other work for her?"

Both her parents stiffened. If Haley didn't work, there was no money for any of them. She had become the Loring paycheck.

The question seemed to hang like a bubble, floating in the air around them. After a long sigh, Sheena had said, "I hate to be blunt, but here it is. Haley is eleven now. As far as being a child star, in this business, she's old."

Her mother had whispered the word, "Old?" just as her father snapped, "That's ridiculous!"

"Look at her," Sheena said grimly. "Her face has lost the adorable roundness. Her nose had lengthened. She's getting tall." Staring directly at Haley, Sheena had added, "Of course, you're getting lovelier by the day, Haley, but ... you're just not cute. Pretty is a whole different look than cute. Cute sells."

Her father had rubbed his chin, like he always did when he was nervous. "Then what's our next move, Sheena? Is it another round of commercials for Haley, or do you have another script for her to look at? We've talked before about getting her into the movies ..."

Tap tap tap. Sheena tapped her black pen against her desk. Finally, she said, "This is difficult. Frankly, I don't have anything for her. I don't anticipate that changing in the near future. Unfortunately, that leaves me with no other choice but to ... terminate Haley as a client."

"What?" Haley had leaped out of her seat. "Sheena, you can't—are you firing me?"

"I'm letting you go."

"But—but we've been together from the start! You said I was the best!" Haley leaned over Sheena's desk as far as she could. Her voice cracked when she added, "You said I was a star!"

Sheena had cooed, "You're absolutely right, you are a star. Everything you ever touched was sprinkled with stardust. But, darling, the world changes. This might be the best thing that could happen to you." Her pen paused in midair as she added, "Now you've got a

7

chance for a new life. A normal life." Staring hard at Haley, she said, "Why don't you just graciously accept that your time has passed and move on?"

"Haley—Ha-leeey!"

The sand was getting colder as Haley made her way toward the tide. A few seagulls screeched overhead. Haley stopped just where the foamy water kissed the sand and felt a rush of tide swell around her ankles. It seemed to pause for just a second before it slipped back into the sea. Looking over her shoulder, Haley saw her parents watching her from the window. Another wave swelled, then crashed and rolled over her feet.

"HA-LEEEY!"

"Alright—I'm coming!" Haley yelled through cupped hands. Couldn't her parents tell that she wanted to be alone? Honestly, Haley thought, sometimes her parents could be so pushy!

Banging the glass door shut behind her, Haley walked into the living room and plopped herself down.

"What?" she asked. "What is so important?"

"Now, listen, young lady," her father began in a warning tone. But as usual her mother interrupted. After shooting her father a "look," Haley's mother said softly, "Sweetheart, we need to talk to you. Now, we wouldn't do a thing without your approval, but, well ... " She cleared her throat. "Your father and I were discussing the possibility of us moving to a nice little town called Garland."

"What?"

"My brother has a lead on a job there," her father continued. "And times being what they are, I think I should take it."

Leaping from her seat, Haley cried, "NO! No way! I do NOT want to move to a town. No. No!"

"Haley, honey, sit down. Your daddy was just making a suggestion."

"It's more than a suggestion!" her father shot back. His jaw twitched. "I know you've had a rough couple of days, but these are the facts. Without 'Family Love,' we can't eat. All of your earnings, and I do mean ALL, are in the bank for your college education. As of right now, this family has zero money."

"Take my money out of the bank," Haley ordered. "We can live off my savings until I've figured out what I'm going to do."

Sighing with exasperation, her father stood in front of Haley and placed a hand on each of her shoulders. "Haley, listen to me. We can't use any of that money. It's in a trust. Your savings can't be touched until you're eighteen! And even if I could get at it, I wouldn't. That money is for your future."

Pulling away from her father, Haley began to pace. The sun was going down, and it cast a rosy glow across the wicker furniture that she'd so carefully picked out the year before. Last year, when she'd had a job. Last year, when her life meant something.

"Okay," she said, holding up her hands. "I've got it. Here's the plan. I'll look around for another agent. There must be plenty of people who'd like to represent me. And then my new agent will get me parts, and we can stay here on the beach. I know I can get work!"

Her mother tried to smile, but Haley could tell she was fighting back tears. Small, dainty features made her mother look younger than she really was. Although her hair was the color of creamed coffee, she'd dyed it to a sunny blond with extra highlights around her face. Today her mother wore tight jeans with leather boots pulled up to the knees and an oversized shirt. Silver charm rings jingled when she moved her hands. She patted the couch for Haley to sit. Reluctantly, Haley dropped beside her mother onto the mint-green couch.

"Sweetheart, why don't you forget about other agents for a while. I think it's time you took a rest from all of this. You've been pulling the cart for so long. Maybe it's time your father and I took a turn."

That's when Haley knew. She could tell by looking into her mother's eyes. They'd already tried to get her another agent, but no one wanted her. Haley felt her insides roll like the sea. Sheena had been right. Her time had passed.

"I think I'd like to go into my room for a while," Haley said softly. "I want to sort this out by myself."

"Sure, honey," her mother told her, giving her a squeeze. "Whatever you want."

Without turning the lights on, Haley crawled across her queen-size bed. Her favorite stuffed animal, a huge white gorilla named Rosie, sat against bubble-gum colored pillows. Haley nestled into Rosie and pulled the animal's long, furry arms around her.

In a voice so soft it barely breathed, Haley whispered, "It's over, Rosie. I guess you and I have to move on."

Two tears rolled down her cheeks and disappeared into Rosie's arms. Her voice cracking, Haley cried, "I just don't know what I'm going to move on to."

"Well, here we are, sweetie! Your new school!" Haley's mother cried in a singsongy voice. "Now, you remember how to get home, don't you? Straight down Melon Drive, a right at Oak Street, and then a left at Orchard. Got it?"

"Yes."

"Great. The principal is waiting for us inside. Are you ready?"

Taking a deep, cleansing breath, Haley looked at the caramel-colored building and shook her head no. She hadn't felt this nervous since she'd auditioned for the Pepsi commercial when she was six. There's nothing to be afraid of, she'd told herself over and over again. But it didn't matter what her little inside voice whispered to her mind. Fear still chilled her like ice.

A cluster of girls with rainbow-colored knapsacks edged against the front of the brick building. Further down, three boys kicked leaves so high they twirled in the air and spun down like clumps of brown snow. The boys looked about eleven years old. They were probably in her new class.

"Hey—dogface, watch this!" a straw-haired boy yelled. He picked up a fistful of leaves and stuffed them into a dark-haired boy's hood. The dark-haired boy yanked them out and threw them on the ground while the blond boy laughed.

Watching them made Haley even more nervous, because although she would be entering the sixth grade, she'd never been a real, true student. In Hollywood all of her tutors had come right onto the set. She'd never had to compete with anyone but herself. Now, she'd just be one little pupil in a class of twenty-eight.

Twenty-eight kids. Her palms began to sweat.

"Haley, you're not moving. Open the car door, sweetheart."

Haley didn't budge.

Her mother reached over and flipped the visor down in front of Haley's face. A small mirror caught her reflection.

"Look at yourself," her mother insisted. "You look positively terrified."

It was true. The grayish blue eyes that stared back looked like two hard-boiled eggs with spots in the middle. Her mouth had white commas at the sides of her lips.

"Honey, I know this is a new experience for you, but I can't understand why you're so scared. They're kids, just like you."

With a flip-flop motion, Haley's stomach began to roll through her middle. She bent over and clutched her sides. "I think I'm going to be sick," she whispered.

"Come on, now, you've done a lot bigger stuff than walking into an elementary school. I don't understand this at all. You've always had amazing confidence—a lot more than I've ever had.''

Haley pushed her hair from her eyes and looked up at her mother. ''Mom, everything else I've done was just pretend. This is for real. What if everyone hates me? I mean if they do, then they'll hate ME, not the character I play! This is different.''

Her mother was quiet for a moment. Finally, she said, ''Haley, no one in that school is a stranger. They're just friends you haven't met.''

Groaning, Haley sat up. Now her mother would start with the chipper mottos, the ones that were supposed to keep Haley pumped up.

''Remember, Haley, you're a star.''

''I WAS a star.''

''No, you ARE a star. And not only that, you're the best.''

A loud bell signaled the children to line up. Teachers appeared out of nowhere to wave them inside the building.

Relieved, her mother said, ''We've got to go now, Haley. Our appointment's in five minutes. We don't want to start off your first day by being late. Turn that frown upside down!''

The words GARLAND ELEMENTARY SCHOOL stood in a bronze row in front of the building. It had rained the night before, so the October colors looked extra bright, as if they'd been highlighted with magic markers. The lawn was blue-green, with tiny bursts of yellow where a few dandelions lingered. Silver bars of the jungle gym caught the rays of the pale autumn sunshine. California air was breezy and warm. Garland air was crisp, and it smelled of bus exhaust, apples, and freshly turned earth mixed with a hint of wood smoke. Shivering, Haley rubbed her bare arms with the insides of her hands.

"I told you that you would need a coat," her mother reminded Haley as she pulled open the door to the school. "Fall means cold. You've been spoiled by the California sunshine. Let's see—there's the front office right over there."

The hallway was polished green tile lined with tan walls. Focus, inhale, smile. Haley stood up straight. If she was scared, no one else needed to know. She didn't want the students of Garland to guess that she was frightened of them, of the school, of the newness of it all. Their footsteps clicked against the floor as they walked, and Haley could hear the pledge of allegiance swell from the different classrooms. They stopped in front of a Formica counter. A round woman in pink gingham sat writing at a desk. Her round cheeks were painted with matching pink circles, and her hair was teased into puffy blond rings. When the receptionist finally looked up, Haley gave her a winning smile.

"Well, Samantha Love, what a pleasure to meet you!" the receptionist cried. "I just have to tell you how much I've enjoyed your show! It's just so exciting to have you here at Garland! Our principal has been waiting for you, and his office is right over there." With the eraser end of a pencil, she pointed to a door with the word PRINCIPAL on it.

"Thank you," Haley said brightly. "And you are . . . ?"

"Me? Oh, I'm Sue Ann Johnson."

"It's nice to meet you, Sue Ann," Haley said, extending her hand. Even though her heart was thumping like a drum, her voice sounded cool and collected.

Sue Ann gave Haley a funny look. She opened her mouth as if to speak, thought better of it, and instead pointed to the office. "Go right in," she said.

"Sweetheart, when you're in an elementary school, you're not supposed to address the adults by their first names," Haley's mother whispered. "You should have called her MRS. Johnson."

"Why? That's not fair!" Haley protested. "She called me by my first name. And it was the WRONG first name, too."

They opened the door to the sound of "Come in, come in, come in!" A thin man jumped up from his desk and shook Haley's hand hard. "I'm Donald Sand, the principal. What a pleasure to have you here at Garland. No one can believe that we'll have a real celebrity among us! Sit down," he said, motioning to a chair. "Would you like a cup of coffee?"

"That would be lovely," Haley's mother said.

"With cream, please," Haley added.

"What?" Mr. Sand stared at Haley, and Haley felt herself color. Maybe this far out in the woods, everyone drank their coffee black.

"Um, if you don't have any cream, black's just fine," Haley faltered.

"Actually, never mind about the coffee," her mother interrupted. "But all of the coffee talk does remind me to give you something. Mr. Sand," Haley's mother said, "Haley would like to donate a small gift." From inside her purse, her mother withdrew a blue mug with the words *Family Love* scrolled inside a heart. The signatures of the show's cast members had been painted on as well.

15

"That's the official mug of the 'Family Love' set," Haley told him.

"This is very nice. I'll put it right on my desk so everyone can see it. Thank you!"

"And thank you for meeting with us like this. I'm sorry Haley had to miss the first three weeks of school, but, with all the details of moving, well, I'm sure you know how it is."

"Perfectly understandable, perfectly understandable. This is going to be quite a wonderful experience for your daughter. Garland has five hundred first-rate students, and we're proud of our staff of talented teachers. We've assigned Haley to Room 103. Her teacher will be Mrs. Walter, and I just need you to go over these forms. Here we are . . ."

As Mr. Sand spoke, Haley's mind wandered the room. It was small and brown, with cheerful, tacky sayings hung all over the walls, like *Make my day, get an "A,"* and *Have you hugged your teacher today?* Mom ought to love those, Haley thought to herself. Handmade knickknacks dotted a shelf, and the principal's sack lunch sat on the edge of his cluttered desk. It was all so different from Hollywood. Instead of coming to another state, Haley seemed to have landed on another planet. How would she face all of those alien kids? What would she say to them?

". . . always made us laugh. Would you?"

A sharp elbow poked Haley in the ribs. It was her mother. Jumping, Haley looked into her mother's wide eyes.

"Mr. Sand would like you to say your Samantha Love line for him." Her mother's voice dripped with the you-weren't-listening-pay-attention tone.

"What? Oh." Haley closed her eyes for a moment and pulled up Samantha's saucy attitude. The fear seemed to vanish as Haley stepped into Samantha's personality. Cocking her head, she flashed a smile and asked, "What's your *prob*-lem?"

Mr. Sand burst into applause. "I know Samantha Love's attitude is, well, not the best role model for kids, but it is just so funny. I love it when she says that! I always wanted to be an actor myself, but I guess I was just too afraid. I have to admit that when I was young, I had an inferiority complex."

"Maybe it wasn't a complex. Maybe you were just inferior," Haley quipped. "I mean, what's your *problem*?"

Slapping his knee, Mr. Sand cried, "Ho, ho, I remember that line from your show. That's very funny, Haley. I can tell Garland is going to be a lot more humorous with you here."

That's when Haley decided that she wouldn't be attending Garland Elementary. She wouldn't have to be nervous. Her stomach wouldn't have to spin. Haley Loring might be too scared to walk into that classroom, but Samantha Love wasn't.

From now on, she would be Samantha Love!

The classroom quieted as Haley entered. Maple desks were lined up in neat rows. Mrs. Walter, a young, round-faced woman with waist-length hair, beamed a smile at Haley and said, "Come in, Haley, we've been waiting for you. Class, this is Haley Loring. Many of you might know her as Samantha Love from 'Family Love.' Welcome!"

Even though Haley's heart was thumping wildly, she tried to make herself look cool and calm. She let her hand flutter through the air, just like Samantha would have done. "Hi!" she said.

"If you wouldn't mind, the class and I would appreciate your telling us a little about your life as an actress, and what it was like growing up in Hollywood." Mrs. Walter squeezed her hands under her chin. "I know I've never met an actress before. This is so exciting for all of us here at Garland!"

Sauntering to the front of the room, Haley leaned against the chalkboard and surveyed the room. Half the girls in the class wore their hair in the exact same way, with their bangs teased into a hair-sprayed puff, while the rest of the hair kinked down their backs. Most of them stared at Haley wide-eyed. One girl let her mouth hang open, and Haley could see a mass of wire inside. The boys gawked, too, but weren't as obvious as the girls were. Some looked at her from underneath their lashes, while others cocked their heads and glanced at her sideways. Two boys in the back row kept punching each other and whispering.

Clearing her throat, Haley reminded herself not to tighten up. It's an acting job, she told herself. Just be Samantha.

"What would you like to know?" Haley asked Mrs. Walter.

"Let's take questions from the class. There's a hand—Bruce, what would you like to ask Haley?"

A boy with a cowlick and freckles looked at Haley, then flushed and slumped in his seat. "I . . . I . . . I don't want to ask anything. I changed my mind."

"I hope your new mind works better than your old one," Haley quipped.

The class roared. Relief rushed through her. They were laughing at that line, just like the studio audience had laughed when she'd said it on "Family Love."

A girl in a pink jumpsuit waved her hand in the air. When Haley pointed to her, she asked, "What was the worst mistake you ever made on your show?"

"The worst mistake I made was when I was supposed to be listening to our dog Bowser's heartbeat with a stethoscope—"

"I saw that show!" a boy cried. "It's the one where you thought Bowser swallowed an alarm clock—"

"Right! That's the episode. Anyway, I was on my

knees, listening to Bowser and going, 'I can hear the clock ticking inside him! Oh, no! Bowser's in trouble!' Except, if you look at the rerun, you'll see that I forgot to put the stethoscope in my ears. It was just hanging around my neck. And there I was, acting like I could hear something! I looked so stupid!'' When the class giggled, she added, ''It's really awful to have your most embarrassing moments caught on film.''

''Have you ever met Dusty Shane of 'California 94109'?'' a girl called out.

''Oh, yeah. He's really nice, but he's a mouth.''

''What's a mouth?'' the girl asked.

''A mouth means he gets really offended if someone talks while he's interrupting.''

A boy with a plaid shirt raised his hand next. ''How much money do you make?''

''Brandon—for heaven's sake,'' Mrs. Walter interrupted. ''You don't ask a question like that.'' She turned to Haley and added, ''Unless, of course, you'd like to tell us.''

Haley raked her fingers through her hair, just the way Samantha did. She pulled it to the top of her head, then let it fall down. ''I earned eight thousand dollars per episode—''

The class gasped.

''But I don't get any of it until I'm eighteen. See, my dad was my manager, and my mom stayed on the set of 'Family Love' and took care of my fan mail and stuff. I paid my mom and dad from my check.''

''You mean, your parents worked for you?'' the plaid boy asked. He looked impressed.

''Yeah. They used to. Anyway, after I paid them, then all the rest of the money went in a trust fund. That means I can't get any of it until college. Right now, I have to beg my parents for an allowance!''

"Did you like the actor that played your brother on 'Family Love'? I mean, his one-liners are so funny.''

Shrugging, Haley said, "One line of dialogue was all he could memorize at a time.''

The class laughed again.

"What do you think of the new girl that replaced you on 'Family Love'?''

That's when Haley lost it. Just for a second. She was no longer Samantha Love, smart and sassy. She was back to Haley Loring, the scared girl who had been fired from her show.

"Candi is okay, I guess.''

"I thought she was darling,'' a girl in blue offered.

"Yes, she is.'' The statement just laid there, like a dog on a hot day. Haley had to think of something, anything, to get past the quietness that seemed to fill the room. She cleared her throat. "It's just, Candi's voice is the worst. I know she's just a little kid, but when she talks, she sounds like Minnie Mouse on helium.''

"Minnie Mouse on helium!'' The class broke into howls of laughter. Some of the boys began to squeak in high falsetto voices. Haley knew she'd won them back.

"Quiet, class, please,'' Mrs. Walter commanded. But even she looked as if she were trying to suppress a smile. "Are there any other questions? Comments?''

" 'Family Love' should have kept you,'' the girl in blue called out.

"Well, I was ready to leave the show. I was tired of the rat race, and I'm really glad I'm here, at Garland Elementary.'' Haley gave a small bow, and the class burst into applause. Mrs. Walter stood and clapped for Haley with her hands stretched out in front of her. "That's just wonderful, Haley," Mrs. Walter said. "Why don't you take a seat in the third row there. We're just beginning a unit on health. Andy, could you please get a *Health and Our World* book for Haley?"

The boy who'd had leaves stuffed down his coat stood and walked to the back of the class.

"Andy is one of our brightest students. If you have any questions, I'm sure Andy would be glad to help. In fact, Andy, why don't you trade places with Cherry? That way you could guide Haley through her first day." Mrs. Walter touched Haley's elbow and walked her to an empty desk next to Cherry's.

"But I wanted to help her, Mrs. Walter!" Cherry protested. Cherry had chocolate eyes and hair the color of sand after the tide washed over it. Her ears were triple-pierced. The studs at the very tips of her ears were tiny cherries. She folded her hands as if in prayer and begged, "Pul-eeeze, Mrs. Walter. Don't make me sit in the front."

"Cherry, you haven't bothered to hand in your last two assignments. We want Haley to know what good students we are here at Garland."

"But Andy's so b-o-r-i-n-g! Haley might go into a coma or something—"

"Cherry! Being a good student isn't boring. Andy, trade places with Cherry, at least for today." Slumping until her chin practically hit the top of her desk, Cherry rolled her eyes at Haley. She made her way to the front of the room, then plopped into a desk that was front row, center. Haley slid into the desk next to the one where Andy now sat and tried not to beam. It had worked. Everyone loved Samantha! Cherry was already fighting over a chance to sit beside her, and the teacher seemed awestruck. The knot in Haley's stomach began to relax. This was going to be easy, she told herself. All she had to do was stay in character.

Perching herself on a tall stool, Mrs. Walter said, "All right, people, please turn to page twenty-three."

"Here." Haley smiled at Andy as he handed her the dog-eared textbook. He didn't smile back. That was odd, Haley thought. She shrugged to herself.

"Now then," Mrs. Walter began, "last Friday we discussed the blood system. Who remembers what carries the blood away from the heart?"

Andy's hand shot straight up. The other kids in the class flipped through their pages, scanning them with one finger.

"Andy?"

"An artery."

"Absolutely right. Very good, Andrew."

"Isn't an artery the place where you go to look at paintings?" Haley asked.

As if on cue, the class laughed. From the corner of her eye, Haley could see Andy stiffen. Mrs. Walter smiled, shook her head and said, "This is just like having Samantha Love in my class. I hope I'm up to it! Now, back to arteries—"

A voice broke in over the intercom. "Mrs. Walter, there's a phone call for you at the office."

"Okay. I'll be right up."

Hopping off the stool, she said, "I'm sorry, class, I've been expecting this call. I'll only be gone about five minutes. Andrew, could you continue asking these questions I've written out here? That way everyone can practice until I get back."

"Sure," Andy replied. He stood and went to the front of the room. Mrs. Walter handed him a book and a piece of paper. She gave his shoulder a pat. "Okay, class, I'll be back."

Andy perched himself on the tall stool. Haley couldn't help but notice that he was pretty cute. His eyes were large and dark, and his chin had a dimple in it. But there was something not quite right about him, and it only took a second for Haley to realize what it was. The white leather hightops that grabbed the stool's rung weren't even smudged. Just pure white, as if they'd been polished. He wore blue jeans, but they looked just-off-the-rack new. His jet-black hair was trimmed to a crisp line, and his skin was so scrubbed that it glowed. Too perfect, Haley thought. He looked like his mother had dressed him.

Clearing his throat, Andy began, "Okay, guys, what does a vein do?"

There was no answer. A boy next to Haley scratched his arm. Two girls in the front began to whisper. Cherry pulled out a mirror and picked through her bangs.

"A vein. What does a vein do? With the blood, I mean."

A boy in a green sweatshirt pulled a comic book from his desk and began to flip through its pages.

"Listen, if an artery carries blood away from the heart, then a vein carries blood . . . where? Where does a vein take it?" He glanced around the room. "Bruce?"

"I—I don't know," Bruce stammered.

"Well, just think a minute. A vein takes blood to the heart. So the definition of vein is—"

"Someone who's conceited," Haley offered.

Twitters filled the air. Andy glared at her and snapped, "Well, seeing as you're from Hollywood, I guess you'd know all about being conceited."

For a split second the class was still. "Oooohhhhh," someone whispered. Haley could feel herself blush. Samantha wouldn't stand for a comment like that, but Haley couldn't think through her old scripts fast enough to come up with a comeback.

Whipping around in her seat, Cherry said, "Just ignore him, Haley. That's what the rest of us do. Hey, I wanted to ask you something—did you get to keep all of your clothes? I mean, when you were on 'Family Love' and you wore that darling red outfit, like, did you get to keep it?"

"Do you have a Mercedes?"

"Did you wear makeup on the show?"

"Does your mom let you date?"

Every face in the class was looking at Haley, smiling, waiting for her to answer. They couldn't see Andy's face. He sat on the stool, twisting the paper in his hand. Before she could answer a single question that had been fired at her, Andy jumped from the stool and waved the book in the air. "Wait a minute, guys," he cried. "We're supposed to be studying!"

This time, Haley was ready for him. In her Samantha voice, she asked, "Hey, Andy, what's your *prob*-lem?"

The class burst into laughter. Andy opened his mouth to speak, but Haley followed up with another Samantha Love line, "What-a-ya-gonna-do?"

Narrowing his eyes, Andy slipped off the stool and sat down at his new desk. Samantha had won.

Even though the bell had rung ten minutes before, the crowd of kids hadn't thinned much. A few had pulled their bikes from the rack, glancing over their shoulders as they pedaled away. But the rest gathered around Haley in a small knot.

"Haley, it is just so supremely cool that you moved to Garland," Cherry bubbled. "Where's your house?"

"Not too far away. I go down Oak and then across Orchard to Maple." Pushing back a cuticle, Haley added, "I picked out that house because it had a big backyard."

Cherry's eyes widened. "You get to decide stuff like where you live? Wow!"

"Yeah, well, Jane and Ben—that's my mom and dad— they taught me to consider the whole picture before I make a selection. They really trust my judgment."

Mindy scuffed her toe through the dirt. A small leaf had caught in her hair-sprayed bangs. "You know," Mindy began, "I was wondering. You're so famous and all. Why on earth did you move here?"

"Well . . . because." She hoped Mindy could tell by the sound of her voice that she wanted to drop it. But the next words out of Mindy's mouth were, "Because why?"

Haley's mind reeled. She hadn't been expecting that question, and there was no way she wanted them to know that her career was already over. Samantha Love was not a loser. "I came to, to take an artistic break. Recharge myself in small-town America, that sort of thing. I've been working since I was two, you know. If I don't like it here, then"—she made a "phhhtt" sound between her lips—"I'm outta here."

"I'd hate for you to leave!" Cherry said. She looked genuinely distressed. "Do you, would you like to come over to my house?"

"Or mine?" Mindy asked.

Pulling her hair to the top of her head, Haley let it cascade down her back in a golden waterfall. "Thanks, guys, but I've got to call my agents and catch up on all sorts of business stuff. Sorry."

"Just one more thing," Mindy asked shyly. "Could I get your autograph?"

"Me, too," Cherry chimed in.

The rest of the group moved forward eagerly. Shaking her head, Haley said, "How about if I do that *mañana?*" When they looked at her blankly, she added, "Tomorrow. That was the word 'tomorrow' in Spanish."

"Oooohhh."

Good grief, Haley thought. The locals are sure easy to impress.

As she walked along a cracked sidewalk, Haley ducked her head to avoid the low-hanging branches. Large trees bent their limbs, so that they almost touched Haley's hair. California trees were scrubby. In Garland, the trees were tall and gnarled, with leaves in every shade of red and gold. She rubbed her arms. The light wind chilled her, and her skin felt cool beneath her fingers. Drinking in the crisp air, Haley felt a surge of energy. Her first day, and she'd made it! Her parents had been right. Living in Garland might be kind of fun.

"Um, Haley Loring? Could you stop?"

Oh, no, Haley groaned. Not more fans!

"Um, could you maybe wait a second? I mean, please?"

Whirling around, Haley saw Andy. And trotting beside him was none other than Bruce what's-his-name, the geek with the freckles.

"Um, hi, Haley," Bruce said. From the "ums" Haley could tell it was Bruce who'd asked her to stop. He beamed at her. Andy looked over her head, then down at the ground. "Um, how 'ya doin'?"

"Oh. Hi." Haley hoped Andy and Bruce didn't want autographs. She really did want to get home.

"Um, how do you feel, I mean, do you like it here?" Bruce stammered. He blushed so deeply all of his freckles disappeared.

"It's okay. For a little school and all." Silence. Bruce just stared, and Andy wouldn't look at her at all. Oh, this is fun, Haley thought. How long was she supposed to wait for Bruce to spit out the words he seemed to be choking on? After a few more seconds, Haley decided to help him out. "Well, bye, got to run."

Waving a wave that she always gave her fans, Haley turned and walked on.

Behind her, she heard a weak "Um, so long."

Oak Lane was a beautiful street, with old red-brick houses, thick ivy, and apple-laden harvest wreaths on almost every door. As she turned onto Orchard, she heard sneakers scuffing through dry leaves. Was it Bruce again? Whirling around, Haley almost ran straight into Andy.

"Jeez, you scared me! Did you need something?" Haley asked.

"I'm just walking home."

"Where do you live?"

Andy narrowed his eyes. "Down the street. Why?"

Holding up her hands, Haley cried, "Whoa! Chill a little. I just wondered."

Shrugging, Andy kicked a pebble. His jaw twitched. Obviously, there was something wrong with him. When he looked at her, Haley noticed he had the kind of eyes where the pupil seemed to swallow up his iris. She'd never seen eyes quite that dark before. He would have been almost cute if his jaw weren't twitching like a rabbit chewing lettuce. What would Samantha do at a time like this? Haley thought about her character and knew instantly that Samantha would confront the problem, especially if the problem was slightly good-looking. Samantha knew how to reach people who weren't centered. "You know, I'm sensing a bit of hostility here."

"Oh, really."

"You're probably bummed because everyone was asking me questions when you were trying to do the vein thing. That happened because it was just my first day here and all. You guys probably don't get many people who are in the Business—that means acting—here."

"It's nothing. Just forget it."

"If you want me to forget something, that means there's something to forget, which means something IS wrong."

With an exaggerated motion, Andy walked around where she stood and continued on down the sidewalk.

"I gotta go," he said.

He looked as perfect from the back as he did from the front. The buttons on his denim jacket winked in the sunlight, and his backpack looked like it had been starched.

That was a change, Haley thought. Everyone else had practically killed themselves to be her friend, and now White Socks here seemed to think he could just leave her standing there. Nobody walked away from her. Skipping a little, she caught up with him.

"Wait a second. It's not like I care or anything, but I am curious. Is the fact that I'm an actress a problem for you?"

"No."

"Did some actress drop you on the head when you were a child?"

"No."

He was walking faster now, and Haley had to pour it on to keep up with him. "Okay, is television against your religion?"

"Just dumb comedies."

Haley felt a direct hit. The critics had said "Family Love" was just a bunch of fluff. Andy must be one of the snobs who didn't like her show. "Oh, I get it. You're more the *National Geographic,* PBS type. You think you're too good for my show."

Now Andy stopped. He was taller than she was, and

he looked down on her as if she were nothing more than an annoying insect.

"Listen, Haley, let's go over a few things about life in Garland." He held up his finger. "Rule number one. When someone is walking AWAY from you, it means they don't want to talk to you. Okay?" He held up a second finger. "Rule number two. It's not because you're an actress that I don't like you. It's because you're obnoxious." Holding up his third finger, Andy finished with, "And rule number three. If you want to talk to somebody, call your agent. I wouldn't mind if you were"—he made the same "phhhtt" sound Haley had made—"outta here." And then, with a wave that looked exactly like the one she'd given Bruce, Andy disappeared into a grove of trees.

What a JERK! Haley couldn't believe it! Here she was, all up because of her success in school, and then this! No one had ever spoken to her that way, not even her parents!

As she walked the rest of the way home, she could hear the *thump-thump* sound her feet made against the sidewalk. Slamming open the front door, she called out, "I'm here. Where are you?"

Scurrying out from the kitchen, her mother came with a dishcloth in her hand. Today her mother had on her Levi's, Color Me Badd sweatshirt, and Reebok sneakers. "Haley, honey, you're back! How was your day? What's wrong?"

Plopping herself onto their couch, Haley kicked off her shoes. "Most of today went great, but on the way home I ran into this guy from my class. I mean, he is so far down on the food chain you can hardly believe it!"

"That's too bad."

"He was rude to me! Right to my face! He said I was obnoxious!"

Her mother sat beside her and smoothed her hair. "He just doesn't know you yet. He's probably just the type of kid who is jealous of someone like you. Forget him."

"Believe me, I'm trying to." Sighing, Haley said, "Well, anyway, I'm hungry. Did you find any bee-pollen yogurt?"

Her mother had pulled her hair into a ponytail, and was twisting it around her finger like a rope. Suddenly, she let her hair slip from her hand.

"Ooops. Haley, I'm sorry. I forgot to go to the store."

"What? But I told you I'd need some yogurt. My energy gets really low this time of day!"

"I know. It's just, when I went to the bank to open an account, well, I met this woman. She's really terrific! On an impulse, we went to lunch, and I had the best time. I'd forgotten what it's like to deal with a real person, instead of people in the business." Jumping to her feet, she said, "I'll run to the store right now and get some."

"It's okay," Haley sighed. "Forget it. I'm just going to lie down for a while."

"Whatever you want," her mother said.

Rosie looked a lot bigger now that she only had a twin bed to rest on. Haley let all of her books drop to the floor as she flopped beside Rosie. "Rosie, you're the only one who'll understand what I'm about to tell you." Rosie looked at her with brown glass eyes.

"This Andy guy, well, he treated me like, like I

wasn't special. I'm scared, Rosie. What if everybody starts to act that way around me? I mean, after awhile, what if no one cares that I was on 'Family Love'? Then what? I don't know if I can stand being a nothing."

Pulling the long stuffed arms around her, Haley tried to squeeze away the feeling that gnawed at her insides. Everyone but Andy loved her. But he was the first crack, the first chip in her armor. Haley prayed he'd be the last.

As they filed into class the next morning, Haley saw a life-sized scarecrow slumped in her seat. "Look, Haley," Cherry cried. "You got Wilbur!"

"What's a Wilbur?" Haley asked.

Mrs. Walter rushed over to Haley, placed her hand on her elbow, and led Haley to her desk.

"This," Mrs. Walter said, pointing, "is Wilbur. He's our Halloween mascot."

"Cute," Haley said. A burlap sack had been painted with a smiling face, then stuffed into the neck of a flannel work shirt. Enormous bib overalls were packed with wads of newspaper. Heavy leather work gloves, work boots, and a hat completed Wilbur's outfit. "Does this mean Wilbur and I will be sharing a seat?"

"Heavens, no, I'll move him out of your desk right away. Wilbur is just a scarecrow I made a long time ago. The first of October, I pull old Wilbur out of storage and move him around the classroom all month long. It helps keep everyone in the Halloween spirit!" With a sweeping motion that encompassed the whole room,

Mrs. Walter said, "I put up more decorations early this morning. This is such a fun holiday!"

Haley looked around her. Orange and black streamers had been entwined from the center of the ceiling to the corners, so that it looked as if a huge spiderweb had swallowed up their classroom. Cutouts of velvet-black cats were taped to each window, and real pumpkins lined the counters. Even the wastebasket had been replaced with one that looked like a cauldron.

"Of course, I'm sure you had a lot more fancy things in Hollywood," Mrs. Walter said. "This is just plain old Garland."

"It looks fabulous," Haley told her. "Really."

From behind, Cherry elbowed her and whispered, "Here comes Andy. Ask Mrs. Walter if I can have my old place back. I want to sit by you!"

But before she had the chance to say anything, Andy brushed by her. "Mrs. Walter, do I still have to sit at Cherry's desk?"

"Haley's only been here one day, and I think she could use a little more help," Mrs. Walter replied. "And Andrew, why don't you take Wilbur to the back of the room so Haley can sit down?"

"Why can't she do it?" Andy protested.

"For heaven's sake, Andrew, help Haley out. You've never been one to shirk responsibility."

Turning, Mrs. Walter walked to the front of the room. At that moment, the final bell rang and the rest of the kids scurried into their seats. That left only Andy and Haley standing. Andy's jaw began to twitch again. He stood, frozen.

"Chop chop, Andy," Mrs. Walter said in a pleasant voice.

The eyes of the class were fixed on Haley and Andy. Trying to hold in a smile, Haley patted Wilbur's straw cowboy hat and said in her sweetest Samantha voice, "Love the clothes, Wilbur. You must be one of Andy's relatives."

As if on cue, the class giggled. Flushing, Andy muttered, "You're real funny. Ever thought of going on television?"

"As soon as Mr. Valdez moves Wilbur, I'll let you all in on a surprise," Mrs. Walter told the class. "Let's go, Andy!"

With a scowl, Andy hoisted Wilbur and set him in the back of the room.

"All right, people, I'm ready to let you in on the news!" Mrs. Walter clapped her hands together like two cymbals. "Eyes up front! I want your attention. This has to do with Halloween!" Haley could see Mrs. Walter's eyes twinkle through her glasses as she took a deep breath. "Well, kids, I did it! We're going to have a dance. A Halloween dance!"

All the girls squealed. The boys groaned.

A dance? Haley's throat tightened. A dance. Garland was going to have a dance.

"Didn't Mr. Sand say we couldn't have one?" Brandon asked. He looked hopeful.

"That was his original opinion. He wanted it to be fair for everyone, regardless of how popular they are."

Cherry snickered and looked over at Bruce.

"But I grew up in Garland with the Halloween dance, and it drove me crazy when my own students couldn't experience it! That dance is a tradition!"

Haley felt her palms begin to sweat. What if no one asked her? Mentally, Haley flipped through all of the fourteen boys in her class. It was possible that one of them might ask her because she had been on television, but it was just as likely that no one would. And then she'd be exposed as a dud to the entire class. It wasn't fair to spring a dance on her when she'd only been there one day! Be cool! she commanded herself. Samantha Love wouldn't care. Picking up her pencil, she began to doodle as if the news wasn't the least bit interesting. But inside, she was shaking.

Mrs. Walter gave a little hop and sat on the edge of her desk. Pumpkin earrings dangled from her ears, and when she moved her head, they swung back and forth like orange gumballs. Beside her, a small clay jack-o'-lantern grinned at the class with jagged teeth.

"Haley, you probably don't understand what's going on here, so I'll explain. When Mr. Sand became principal awhile back, he decided that too many kids got left out in a traditional dance situation. Consequently, the sixth grade class hasn't had a dance in three years. But I was sitting in the teacher's lounge last week, when"— she snapped her fingers—"I got an idea! What if the girls put their names into a bag, and then the boys drew partners? That would be completely fair. And we've got a real bonus because of you, Haley."

"Because of me?"

"Now that you're here, the class is evenly divided between boys and girls. When I explained my idea to Mr. Sand, he said yes! We'll have it in the gym, just the way we used to, and each pair will come in costumes as a couple. I'm absolutely THRILLED!"

The room began to buzz. Some of the kids looked excited, but Haley couldn't help but notice that the ones

37

who seemed happiest were also the kids who probably wouldn't have been asked to a regular dance.

Cherry's hand cut through the air like a flag. "Wait a minute. I have a question. Are you saying we won't have a choice of who we'll get to go with?"

"Think of it as a lottery," Mrs. Walter offered. "It will be all up to chance!"

"What if I hate the girl I pick?" a boy named Chase asked. "Can I trade?"

The smile vanished from Mrs. Walter's face. "Absolutely not. The person whose name you pick is the person you'll go to the dance with, period. And to make sure no one trades, I'll keep a master list. If ANYONE tries to make a swap, they'll get an *F* in Social Studies. Got that? Now then, since the dance is less than two weeks from now, there's no time like the present to begin our drawing. Boys, I want you to line up against the wall. That's the way."

Moaning and ducking their heads, all the boys lined up. Mrs. Walter produced a plastic pumpkin and rattled it around.

"The names of all the girls in our class have been placed into this pumpkin."

Raising her hand, Mindy called out, "Is Haley's name in there?"

"Of course. Now, boys, part of the fun will be HOW you ask your partner to the dance. Try to be original. Don't reveal who you are until you actually invite the girl in your own special way. The deadline for your invitations is this Friday. And girls"—she took on her warning tone again—"I don't care WHO you get. If I even hear that you were anything but gracious, I'll flunk you." Turning back to the line, she said, "You boys are almost teenagers. When inviting your date, try and act your age.''

Chase clutched his hands over his heart and batted his eyelashes. In a falsetto voice, he pleaded, ''Please come with me to the Halloween dance. I always wanted to take a witch!''

''Cut the smart stuff, Chase,'' Mrs. Walter said. ''Now, let's begin. Tom, come on up and pick.''

A skinny boy with braces rolled his eyes and clumped to the front of the room. With a sigh, he reached into the pumpkin and pulled out a piece of paper. He unfolded it quickly, read it, and jammed it into his pocket. Haley could tell by the look on his face that he was pleased with his date.

''Let me see that paper so I can write down who you got.'' Tom dug it out of his pocket and showed it to Mrs. Walter. Mrs. Walter read the name and smiled at Tom. ''That's great! I'm sure the two of you will have fun.''

Kissing noises filled the room.

''All right, Chase, you're next.'' Mrs. Walter stretched the pumpkin toward him. Chase dug around for a minute, then pulled out a piece of paper. When he read it, he looked directly at Haley and grinned.

Chase? Would Chase be the one? Haley felt her stomach squeeze. But when Chase sat down, he flashed a smile at Mindy, so Haley wasn't sure.

A note skittered across Haley's desk. Dropping it into her lap, she read,

''Haley, wanna bet I get Andy? The only one worse would be Bruce. The guys you want to get are Chase, David, Brandon, and maybe Kenneth. Do you think this is fun?''

On the back of the note, Haley wrote,

"It depends on who I get. If it's the wrong guy then I think I feel a case of the flu coming on. My parents would back me all the way!"

The note came back again with the words "You're so lucky" scrawled across it.

"Bruce, it's your turn," Mrs. Walter said. Eagerly, Bruce dove at the pumpkin. He squeezed his eyes shut and removed a name. Walking over to his teacher, he showed it to her but didn't read the name himself. "I'll look at it later, when I'm alone," he explained.

One by one, the boys dipped their hands into the pumpkin. Most of them squirmed around and made faces to show they were absolutely miserable, but Haley could tell they were into it. All except Andy. He looked like he'd been cast in cement. The last one in line, Andy walked up to the pumpkin and shoved his hand inside.

"This is easy for you, Andrew. You've got the very last name. I'm sure good things come to those who wait."

When he read his piece of paper, his face kept the same stony expression.

"Who did you get?" Haley called out. "Wilbur?"

The class twittered. If looks could kill, Haley would have been a goner.

Almost everyone at Garland took a hot lunch. Eleven pink, yellow, and blue plastic trays made a rectangle around the place Haley sat, except for the empty spaces she'd saved for Mindy and Cherry. The girls in her class had fought for the chance to sit by her. Three of them had already changed their hair so that it hung loosely, exactly as Haley's did. A girl named Grace came to school in an outfit that looked like the one Haley had worn the day before, but her earrings were wrong.

"Um, hi, Haley," Bruce said. He clutched a cafeteria tray in his hands, and when he swallowed, his Adam's apple bobbed. Haley didn't know that a kid that young could even get an Adam's apple.

"Hi."

"Do you like tacos? They're usually good, but today they smell kind of funny."

"I'm a vegetarian."

Blushing, Bruce said, "Oh. I didn't know. Um, bye." Then he moved on to the table where all the boys sat.

Haley leaned into the table and declared, "With a nose like that I bet he smells everything funny."

The girls around her howled. Every time she said a line from "Family Love," they laughed harder than the studio audience ever had. But in a lot of ways, being Samantha Love full-time was more work than Haley had expected. Smart and sassy, Samantha Love always kept people in their place with withering one-liners. These girls demanded that she be cool and witty at all times, and Haley knew she couldn't let them down. The only problem was, Haley Loring of Garland didn't have a writer to compose her lines. One thing's for sure, Haley thought to herself, real life is a lot tougher than just acting a script.

She opened her sack lunch with yogurt, tofu salad, and Chinese cucumber sticks. Haley tried not to smell the tacos, which were making her mouth water. The woman who'd played her mother on "Family Love" had taught her to be a strict vegetarian.

"I think I'll bring a sack lunch tomorrow," Grace said as she watched Haley pull the lid off her yogurt.

A chorus of "Me, too" followed.

"I'm always careful of what I eat," Haley explained. "People worry more about what they put into their cars than about what they put into their bodies."

Just then, Cherry breezed into the cafeteria, grabbed a tray, and let it clatter down beside Haley.

"You'll never believe it!" Cherry said, sliding into place. "I just came from the girls' room. Now, if I tell you guys this, you've got to PROMISE you won't tell that I told you. Really. Mindy made me absolutely SWEAR that I wouldn't tell. But I've just got to say it!"

"What's going on?" Haley asked.

Cherry took a gulp of air. She looked around the table, then dropped her voice low. "You guys swear?"

They all nodded.

"Okay. It's about the dance. You'll never believe it in a million years. Try and guess who Mindy got!"

"Chase," Haley said. She took a bite of tofu.

Cherry's jaw opened so wide that Haley could see a black filling. "How did you know? Haley, how did you guess that?"

"An actress studies people. I could tell by the way he moved that it was Mindy. How did he ask her?"

"Well, he walks up to her and goes, 'Mindy, I got the short straw. I guess we're going together.' And then she goes, 'I guess if I have to.' That was it! Cute, huh?" Clutching Haley's knee, Cherry cried, "Oh, here she comes! Now, when Mindy tells you, act like you don't know. She'll kill me if she finds out I told you first."

Almost skipping, Mindy snatched the last tray from the counter and ran to the table. "Hi, guys! Hey, scoot over. There's hardly any room."

The line of girls on Haley's right wiggled over, and Mindy dropped into a place. She must have squirted something on herself in the bathroom, because Haley's eyes began to water from the strong scent of lily of the valley. Mindy's short brown hair whipped through the air whenever she turned her head, which seemed to be after every sentence.

"Thanks for saving my place, Haley." When she saw Cherry sitting on Haley's left side, Mindy narrowed her eyes. "Did Cherry tell you my news?"

Haley made her face a complete blank. "News?"

"About the dance. Did she tell you?"

"I have no idea what you're talking about. Cherry and I were busy eating. Would you like some tofu?"

Satisfied, Mindy gave a little bounce. "Well, anyway, guess what?" She bubbled. "You'll never guess in a gazillion years! I got asked to the dance by Chase! CHASE! Can you believe it?"

And just as if she hadn't already known, Haley widened her eyes and straightened her back. "Chase? You're kidding me! Incredible!"

Cherry shot her a grateful look. I'm an actress, Haley thought. That was easy.

Mindy pulled her napkin off her tray, and a spoon and fork clattered across the Formica tabletop. "Ooops! Sorry—I'm just so excited, I'm about ready to die! And I've got some more news." She leaned forward so that she could see around Haley. "Cherry, I think I know who got your name. Chase told me."

"Oh my gosh, oh my gosh, who?" Cherry shrieked. "Tell me!"

Shaking her head, Mindy said, "Well, before I say it, I want you to prepare yourself. It's not good."

"Just TELL me!"

"I'm not one hundred percent positive because it was Chase who—"

"Mindy, either you tell me right now or I'll lose this taco on your lap."

"It's Bruce."

At the sound of his name, Cherry deflated. After a minute, she crossed her arms and smirked. "I know what you're doing. It's a joke, right? I mean, my luck's not that bad."

"It's for real. Chase said he watched Bruce unfold it in the boys' room." Letting her fork drift through her

44

peas, Mindy said, "You know, life can be funny some-times."

"I don't believe it. I don't BELIEVE it!" Cherry crushed an empty milk carton with her fist. "I got BRUCE? This is so darned UNFAIR!"

Like a wave, the girls' heads rippled together from one end of the table to the other. Names of people Haley didn't know floated around. There were whispers of boys and places, things and people she couldn't connect to. She'd become invisible. Garland had a history she didn't know a thing about, and in an instant she'd be-come an outsider. She took another bite of food. It was strange, Haley thought, the way food could turn into a lump in your mouth. When she swallowed, it felt as though a baseball was passing down her throat.

"My sister went with Kenneth's brother the very last time they had it," Grace told another girl.

"Really? They're still together, right?"

"Uh-huh."

Cherry and Mindy were arguing over who had the most luck.

"You were the one who won that big Winnie-the-Pooh teddy bear. I really wanted that thing, but YOU won it!" Mindy argued. "It's my turn to get lucky."

"We were in second grade! Besides, YOU were the one who got the free pass to the water slide."

"YOU were the one who found three dollars on Hud-son Hill," Mindy countered.

Shaking her head, Cherry said, "It doesn't matter what you say, it's obvious. You're lucky and I'm CURSED. If you want proof, then notice that YOU get Chase and I get Bruce!"

What would Samantha do? She'd take charge. She

45

wouldn't allow herself to be ignored. She'd jump right in with all the answers!

"Now wait a minute," she commanded. "Calm down."

All the girls quieted. Holding a cucumber as if it were a pointer, Haley declared, "This is simple. Cherry, you don't want to go with Bruce? Then don't go with him. You can fight this thing."

"Right," Cherry snorted.

"I mean it! I think being ASSIGNED to a guy for a dance is like, from the Dark Ages. I'd even bet it's unconstitutional. Why don't you call a lawyer and sue the school or something?"

Cherry blinked, hard. Her eyebrows knit together in a line. "What? You're in Garland, Haley. That legal stuff won't fly out here. If a teacher says we're going, we're going."

A few of the girls snickered. Obviously, the lawsuit idea was a mistake. The off-balance feeling welled inside Haley. In Hollywood, if there was a problem, the first thing you did was call a lawyer. She felt her power slip.

From the end of the table, a chubby girl in yellow asked, "You got any more great ideas?"

"Well, you can always act sick."

For the first time since Haley had known her, Cherry looked annoyed. "Maybe that will work for you, but it's not that easy for the rest of us. My parents can always tell when I fake it. They'd never believe me if I all of a sudden said I felt pukey."

"There's more to faking than just saying you're sick."

"Like what?"

Every girl at the table leaned forward, intent on Haley's every word.

"You ACT," Haley said. "I mean, come on, guys. Squeeze a little Visine in the eyes so it looks like you've been crying. Moan, like this."

Clutching her sides, Haley let out a low moan and doubled over. "Ooh, I'm so sick." She grabbed her head, and squeezed it between her fingertips. "My head is POUNDING! I think it was the tacos I ate at school. The room is going round and round and round. I'm hot and cold at the same time. Ohh, I think I'm going to throw up."

She felt a hand on her shoulder. When she looked up, she saw Mr. Sand's concerned face inches from her own.

"Are you all right, Haley?" he asked. His face was so close, she could smell the coffee on his breath. "Do you need to go home? You're white as a sheet!"

"I—I'm okay," Haley puffed. "I—I think I feel a little bit better now. It's just my stomach." She let out another whimper.

"Should I call your mother?"

"No. Please, let me stay. I don't want to miss any school." She gripped Mr. Sand's forearms. "Just give me a moment. I'll get better, really."

"Nonsense. If you're ill . . ."

"No, just let me try." With three shallow pants, then a deep breath, Haley righted herself. Mr. Sand smoothed the hair at the top of her head.

"I'm better now," she said weakly. "Thank you."

He hesitated. Haley gave him a forced smile.

"You've got a lot of dedication," Mr. Sand told her. "Most of these other girls would have called it quits

47

and gone home by now. You girls could learn a thing or two from Haley.''

''Absolutely,'' Cherry said.

Her eyes innocent, Grace added, ''We've already learned so much from her, Mr. Sand.''

''For sure. We're impressed!'' Mindy exclaimed.

The rest of the girls nodded solemnly at their principal.

''Now, Haley if you feel you need to go home, please, come right into my office and I'll call your mother myself. You take care, Haley.''

''I will. Thanks, Mr. Sand.''

As Mr. Sand walked on, Haley let her face clear. She picked up her spoon and stuck it into her yogurt. Twisting it, she looked around the table and smiled. ''See what I mean? It's all in the delivery.'' She took a bite and added, ''If you claim food poisoning, then you don't have to come up with a fever.''

''Super! Haley, you were fantastic!'' Cherry squealed.

''I never do anything I don't want to do.''

Mindy, her voice filled with awe, added, ''I can't believe you fooled Sand.''

''Amazing,'' Grace said reverently.

''I'm a professional.''

The girls at the table looked impressed. Haley felt her balance returning. She was back in the center, where she needed to be.

Samantha Love was in control.

"**H**i, Mom, I'm home. Day two in Garland Elementary is officially over. Mom?"

From around the corner, her mother appeared, holding a cordless phone. She held up one finger and signaled Haley to wait.

"Is that about me?" Haley asked. She pointed to the phone and then to herself. Her mother shook her head no and continued talking.

"Sure. We'd love to come. Thanks so much for thinking of us, Rita. Six-thirty sounds great. Bye."

Pushing the antenna back into the phone, her mother turned to Haley. "Sweetheart, hello. How was school?"

"Okay. Except I have to go to some stupid Halloween dance with some guy I don't know. It was my teacher's lame idea that the class draw names out of a plastic pumpkin. I'll find out who got me in the next couple of days."

"That sounds kind of fun," her mother offered.

"It depends on who I get. If it's a geek, then I'm NOT going."

"Of course not!" Her mother followed Haley into the kitchen. She opened up the refrigerator, an old white one with rounded corners, and poured Haley a glass of juice. Their kitchen was completely different from the one in California. The Garland kitchen seemed squat, with old-fashioned ruffled curtains and maple cabinets. In California, everything had been done in white and mint, with crisp lines and gleaming chrome. Haley thought the Garland kitchen seemed tired from all the breakfasts, lunches, and dinners it had served.

"Were there any calls for me today?" Haley asked.

"Nope."

"Who were you on the phone with?"

"A friend of mine. We've all been invited over to her house for dinner tonight." Her mother set the apple juice on the countertop, then dropped onto a stool beside her daughter. "I told her we'd be there around six-thirty. Is that a problem?"

Sighing a long sigh, Haley said, "It's okay. It's just that I'd like you to ASK me, instead of TELL me. And exactly who is this person?"

Her mother picked up a napkin and wiped a quarter-sized spill off the counter. Haley noticed three of the charm rings were missing. The jeans she wore were her old loose pair, and she didn't have her skin foundation on, which meant Haley could see enlarged pores on her nose. A few days in Garland, and her mother was beginning to let herself go.

Folding the napkin as she talked, her mother said, "Do you remember that woman I told you about? The one from the bank?"

"Sort of."

"Well, her name is Rita, and she's very down to

earth. I like her a lot. She's married, with a couple of kids, she runs a bank, and she manages to keep it all together somehow. She's the first friend I've made here, Haley.''

"And you want me to be extra nice so I don't scare your new buddy away.''

With a smile that was halfway between a grin and a grimace, her mother said, "I'm asking you to be your own charming self. Okay?''

"All right, Mom, I'll be on my best behavior.''

"I'm serious, Haley. No Samantha Love tonight. I get the idea that Rita runs a tight ship.''

Grinning, Haley said, "Hey, no *prob*-lem!''

It was already dusk by the time Haley's father walked in the door. "Hurry, Ben,'' her mother cried. "We don't want to be late. I don't even know where Rita lives! I think it's close but I'm not sure, and we could drive in circles if we can't read the street signs. How do I look?'' Her mother had on a pair of black pants, a black turtleneck, black shoes, and a black bow. She hadn't put on her usual loopy jewelry, and her hair had been smoothed into a tight ponytail.

"You look like a Ninja,'' Haley offered.

"Thank you, Haley. Just what I needed to hear to feel confident.''

"You look great, honey. Calm down, we'll find it.'' Her father loosened his tie and asked, "How's my girl? Civilian life okay for you?''

"It's strange. Weird. I feel like I should be going to work every day or studying my lines or something, you know?''

Her father gave her a bear hug that lifted Haley's feet

51

all the way off the ground. He used to smell like Fabergé For Men, but now he smelled like Prell shampoo and cinnamon tic tacs. He kissed the top of her head and said, "I know exactly what you mean. I still think I should be calling someone to do lunch. When I'm driving, I keep reaching for my car phone, but there's no one to call. It's different here." He gave her head a final kiss. "But I like it."

"Me, too!" her mother echoed.

Haley didn't say a word. Her parents didn't ask.

"Fourteen-seventy-two Walnut Drive," her mother read from the index card. "I think you turn left here. My word, look at that. It's right around the corner from us!"

The houses that lined Walnut Drive were bigger than the ones on Haley's street. Although the lawns showed the dusty green of fall, they were still closely clipped, with the leaves swept as if by a giant vacuum cleaner. A few paisley-shaped mounds of earth held marigolds, their blossoms shadowy under a half-moon just beginning to shimmer through the treetops. Looking up, Haley could see a few pale stars.

"I smell smoke," Haley said.

"It's from a chimney. Isn't it great to smell wood smoke instead of smog?" her father replied. He smacked his chest with his fist. "Back to basics! Fruit orchards, clean air, plenty of sunshine—that's what's so good about Garland!"

"And we can kill our own food with our bare hands and wear the hides on our feet for shoes!" Haley added.

Pursing her lips, her mother warned, "Haley!"

"It was just a comment. Is that the house there?"

Haley strained to read number fourteen-seventy-two in brass scroll.

"That's it. Let's all be extra nice, okay?" As her mother rang the doorbell, a chime echoed through the house.

"Jane, come in! I'm so glad you could join us. My husband, Michael, is in the kitchen finishing up, so he'll be right out. And you must be Ben. Hello!" A fortyish woman with jet-black eyes shook Haley's father's hand. She definitely seemed different from the people her mother usually hung around with. For one thing, Rita didn't wear makeup, and for another thing, her hair had little streaks of gray. The Hollywood women always dyed their hair.

"And of course, I recognize you. It's a pleasure to meet you, Haley." Rita grasped Haley's hand and gave it a firm squeeze. "I haven't seen many of your shows, but I've always admired your acting."

"How nice of you to say that. Thank you for inviting us," Haley replied. She glanced around at the Victorian furnishings. Everything in the house was done in a deep rose and forest green. The legs of the furniture were the kind that had little claw feet at the bottom, and the wooden floor was polished until it gleamed. "You have a charming home."

"Why, thank you, Haley. It's refreshing to see such a poised young lady. Let me introduce you to my youngest son." Leaning around the corner, she called, "It's time to meet our surprise guest." She turned back and told Haley in a low voice, "I know your being here will knock him right over. He's such a fan of yours that I thought it would be fun to just watch his reaction."

Haley put on her enchanting smile, the one she used

for interviews. But when Rita's son rounded the corner, Haley's lips froze.

In his crisp, white shirt and ironed socks, it was none other than Andy Valdez.

It took only a second for Haley to compose herself. She extended her hand and gave Andy a firm handshake. "Your mother tells me you're a big fan of mine! I didn't know that—thanks a lot!"

With a veneer of a smile, Andy returned her handshake. His hair had just been washed, and his skin was polished clean. When he talked, it seemed as if his words were being squeezed through his teeth. "I really didn't know the surprise guest was Haley Loring. Mom, I sure wish you'd told me who it was."

"I wanted it to be a special treat! These are Haley's parents, Mr. and Mrs. Loring."

"Hello," Andy said. "It's nice to meet you."

Knitting her eyebrows together, Haley said, "I'm not sure, but I think we're in the same class at school. You have Mrs. Walter, right?"

It was surprising, the way Andy could answer without missing a beat. He squinted at the corner of the room, as if deep in thought, and said slowly, "Wait—I think I remember you. Don't you sit near the back?"

"For heaven's sake," Andy's mother interjected. "How could you miss Haley? You've been talking about how cute she is for years!"

"M-o-m!" Andy cried. His eyes were so wide, they looked like they'd pop right off the side of his head.

"I'm sorry, I think I'm embarrassing my son. How about if the adults go into the living room, and you two kids can get acquainted."

"But—" Haley was about to say she didn't want to be herded off like a cow down a trail, but her mother flashed her a pleading look.

"Is that all right with you, sweetheart?" her mother asked.

"Sure. Fine." Haley crossed her arms and tried not to look at Andy.

"Oh, Andy," Mrs. Valdez said. "Did you finish setting the table?"

"Yeah, it's done."

A deep voice, one that sounded a note above a baritone, rumbled up from the hallway. "Except you forgot to set the napkins." A square, balding man came in, wiping his hands on a towel as he spoke. "Hello, I'm Michael Valdez. It's a pleasure to meet you folks." After shaking hands all around, he announced, "In honor of the chill in the air, I've made hot toddies. They're right this way. And son"—he turned to Andy— "the water glasses need to be set, too. Never leave a job half done."

"Sorry, Dad."

The two of them were left standing in the hallway. "Come on." Andy sighed. Haley tried to stifle a grin as she followed him into the dining room.

The table had been set with bone china and silver. A

dozen red roses bloomed from a vase, and a thick Irish lace tablecloth skimmed velvet chairs. The silverware had been set in perfect geometric lines. Andy went to the china hutch and pulled out crystal goblets.

Sauntering over to the table, Haley picked up a plate. She could see herself reflected in its surface.

"Excuse me," Andy said. Haley put down the plate and moved to the side. She heard a plunk, and then another plunk. Andy was setting the goblets with a vengeance.

"By the way," he said. Plunk. "Just so you know." Plunk. "My mom was mixed up." Plunk. "I liked a different girl on a different show. She never watches television, so she got it wrong." Plunk. "I mean, I never said you were cute or anything."

Nodding, Haley said, "That's okay. I never said you were cute, either."

A tiny edge of a grin flickered at the corners of Andy's mouth, but it vanished almost as quickly as it appeared. From a drawer, Andy produced creamy linen napkins that he folded into perfect rectangles. He seemed to be ignoring her, so Haley wandered the room and let her hand drift across the backs of the furniture. The material shifted its feel under her fingertips; cool silk, soft velvet, the nub of brocade, smooth cotton. She peered into the lighted hutch. Silver picture frames held photos of the Valdez family. A small Andy and an older brother, who looked exactly like Andy, except his ears stuck out, were clutching fishing poles as they sat in a canoe.

"Who's that with you in the boat?" Haley asked.

"My brother, James. And it's a canoe."

57

"I like the ears. With those suckers, I bet he could hear the fish blink."

In spite of himself, Andy gave a little laugh. "He's in high school now, and they don't look so bad. I used to call him Radar, until one day he said he didn't like it and he pounded me. He's not here tonight because he's at basketball practice."

"Hmm. Is that you in the red wagon?"

Andy set down the last napkin and walked over to the hutch.

"Yeah, that's me."

"Is that you holding the blue ribbon?"

Andy moved closer. His breath smelled like peppermint, and when he moved his arm, his hand brushed against her skin.

"That one over there"—he pointed to an eight-year-old with a huge grin—"that's me. The one on the left is Radar. We both won for our science projects that year. And that's me when I won the spelling bee in fourth grade."

The picture showed a boy with big front teeth holding up a small gold trophy.

"And way back there is me when I had my first violin lesson—"

Shaking her head, Haley said, "Wait a minute. You won the spelling bee, the science fair, AND you play the violin, too? Jeez, Valdez!"

"What?" He peered at her more closely. "What?!?"

Before she could answer, Andy's father appeared at the door. He surveyed the table. "Nice job, Andrew," he said. "Now I'd like you to give the salad a final toss. We'll be sitting down to eat in about one minute.

Haley, would you mind pouring the water in the goblets? The pitcher is right there on the table."

"Me?"

"Yes, if you would."

"Sure," Haley answered. She smiled as if it were a real pleasure, but inside she felt a surge of irritation. What was this, anyway? Did they think that because she and Andy were young, that meant they were free labor? Ever since she'd been there, she'd watched Andy work like a slave, and now they expected her to do it, too. It was unbelievable!

When her parents filed into the room, Haley was just finishing up with the final glass. She gave them a small curtsy, as if she were a French maid, but they just smiled back at her. The sarcasm, Haley decided, was definitely wasted.

When she'd seen Andy at the beginning of the evening, she'd thought dinner was going to be a chore. But it was actually fun. The food was delicious, her parents seemed relaxed, and Andy was actually funny. He kept telling stories about a kid he had to baby-sit who liked to hide things down the heater vents. For being so starched on the outside, he was pretty easygoing in his own home. The only shadow on the evening was the way her mother watched Rita's every move. It was as if her mother thought Rita was another life form.

"It looks like everyone's finished," Rita said when Haley's father had taken his last bite. "Let me just clear these, and I'll be right back with coffee." In a flash, she'd stacked all of the plates and whisked them away, only to reappear with a silver coffeepot. "This is decaffeinated. Would you care for some? And while I'm pouring, Andrew, would you please bring out the chocolate cake?''

''Sure. Want me to put it on plates?''

''That would be wonderful.''

''Haley,'' her mother hissed. She jerked her head toward the kitchen, and for a moment, Haley wondered if her mother had developed a tic. Finally, her mother announced, ''I'm sure Haley would like to help, too. Go on, sweetheart.''

Help? Haley narrowed her eyes and shot her mother a look, but her mother shot one right back. Samantha Love would have made an interesting suggestion on what to do with the cake, but Haley swallowed the words. Blinking hard, she said, ''Absolutely. I'd love to.''

She pushed away from the table and followed Andy into the kitchen. As the door shut behind them, she heard Rita say, ''He's always been terrific. Michael and I firmly believe in giving our children responsibility . . .''

Wonderful, Haley thought. Her mother had made friends with a dictator.

Andy was already kneeling on the counter. ''I'll get down the plates,'' he told her.

Even though the kitchen was roughly the same size as the one in the Loring house, Haley couldn't help but notice how much nicer the Valdez kitchen looked. They'd remodeled it with new appliances, cherrywood cabinets, and pouffy window curtains. A lamp that hung over the kitchen table was etched with roses. The floor was vanilla-colored tile, and in the corner stood a large wicker basket filled with silk daffodils.

''This is nice,'' Haley said.

''My mom loves to decorate. Watch out, don't drop

these." He handed a stack of plates that matched the china on the table.

"Before we go back in there, I have a question." Haley set the plates on the counter. "Have you ever seen the movie called *Children of the Pod?*"

"Nope."

"Well, it's a dumb movie about these aliens that come to earth in these pod things and take over the bodies of kids, and then the kids become perfect robots for their families."

Andy hopped down, opened the refrigerator, and withdrew a two-layer chocolate cake.

"Wait a minute," he said, setting the cake on the counter. "I think I did see that one on the Late Late Show. Don't their beds turn into pea pods, and then they spray pollen on their parents and then take them over, too?"

"Yeah," Haley said. "That's the one. Anyway," she continued, "I have this feeling that I should check out your room. I think I might find a pod."

Andy pulled a knife from a butcher block. "What's that supposed to mean?" he asked.

"Don't get mad. It's just watching you, well, it's really . . . different."

"Different how?"

"I don't know. I mean, my brother on 'Family Love' was the good kid, and the writers had to include a few bad things every once in a while to make sure his character stayed believable. But you." She shook her head. "I think your parents should lock their door at night to make sure you don't rise up and give them a pollen shower."

"Listen, I'm not like that."

"Yes you are. You're a straight-*A* student, and your clothes are so clean you could do a soap commercial. You do exactly what your parents tell you to the second they tell you to do it. Plus, you play the violin." She made her arms into a cross and backed up a few steps. "It's *Children of the Pod* all over again! Don't spray me—please, don't spray me!"

Andy turned and stuck the knife in the cake. He didn't say a word. After a minute, Haley shifted her weight to her other foot. Was she supposed to just stand there, watching him? The feeling that she should have shut up about five minutes ago began to creep over her. Drat, she thought, now he's mad. She definitely shouldn't have said the pea pod thing. So what? Haley argued with herself. What did it even matter what he thought of her? It wasn't like they were friends or anything. She bit the side of her lip. A clock on the wall ticked quietly, and the sound of her parents' voices drifted through the door. She felt stupid just standing there, but she didn't want to go, either.

One by one, he took slices of cake and carefully set them on the plates. She wished he'd say something. He was probably thinking she shouldn't have criticized him. He was probably thinking what a big mouth she had, and how he wished she'd never come over. He probably hated her. Maybe he guessed that she'd never been around kids her own age. In Hollywood, she'd had a lot of people hovering around her, but they'd always been adults. Sheena had been the closest thing to a friend she'd ever had. Even at Garland, she was Samantha Love, and Cherry and the others were her audience.

Finally, he looked up and cleared his throat. Haley felt her stomach flip-flop. One thing acting had taught her was how to read people, and she knew he was going to tell her off.

"Do you remember that episode you did about the Halloween trick with the fishing pole?" he asked.

"The one where I used the violin bow?" That wasn't exactly what she'd thought he was going to say. She felt her face scrunch up in a question mark.

"Yeah. Was that for real? I mean, would it work?"

"I think so. We did it on the set, but the set had real windows. Now that I think about it, I'm sure it would work. Why?" A beat later, she added, "I thought you never watched my show."

"Well, maybe I did, a little. I thought that one was funny." Andy licked a smudge of chocolate off his finger. "After we give them the cake, do you want to try it out? It's dark outside. Do you dare?"

"Sure." And then, louder, she added, "Sure!" He wasn't mad at her. He'd even watched her show and liked it a little. And for some strange reason, having Andy like her mattered a lot.

Frost was beginning to form on the grass. It crunched beneath their feet as they made their way around the side of the house. "Stay down," Andy whispered.

"I AM!" Haley hissed.

Crouching low, with a fishing pole in hand, Andy scurried to the window and peeked inside. Their parents were still sitting exactly where they'd left them moments before. After Andy had served them the slices of cake, he'd said, "Haley and I don't want any cake, so is it all right if we watch a movie?"

Haley's mother had looked up in surprise. "A movie? Sure," she'd said. At the same moment, Rita had asked, "Which one did you want to see?"

"The Snowman."

"Don't forget it's a school night and it's already"— she'd glanced at her watch—"eight o'clock. How long is the movie?"

Shrugging his shoulders, Andy had said, "I don't know. About an hour."

Haley's father had taken a bite of cake and said,

"Well, that sounds fine to me," at the exact time Michael had asked, "Andrew, do you have any homework?"

Both Haley and Andy shook their heads no.

"So can we?" Andy had persisted.

Haley's parents had looked over at Rita and Michael, who'd nodded their permission. Andy led Haley out of the living room and down a hallway.

"Do you have to get a note signed when you want to use the bathroom?" she'd asked him. "Sheesh."

"Sometimes it feels like it. The family room's right in here." He flipped on the lights. The furniture looked cozy, with an overstuffed couch and a rocking chair with a country quilt draped across it. Haley noticed that the Valdez television set was a lot smaller than the one in her home.

In a low voice, he'd told her, "I'll grab the *Snowman* tape and put it in, and then I'll sneak into my room and get my stuff. You still want to try it?"

"Sure, if you do." She'd dropped into the chair and rocked back and forth. Andy scanned a bookcase full of videos.

"You know, in California, I had a movie system right in my room with speakers hooked up to a big-screen TV and everything."

"Uh-huh."

"Now that we're in Garland, Dad put all my stuff in the family room. He says it's still mine and I can take it when I go to college."

"Wow. Just a second, I can't find the tape." Andy had run his finger along the row of movies. His lips had moved as he read the titles, searching for the right one.

"See, I used to have a great big bedroom." She'd

held her hands out to her sides. "I'm talking even bigger than my parents' room, and I used to have a queen-sized bed and a stereo, PLUS a computer." She'd sighed, waiting for Andy to comment on her past riches. Then she'd added, "The homes out here have teeny-tiny bedrooms, so my things got all spread out through the rest of our place. But they're still mine."

"Okay, here it is!" Andy had cried, pulling a video from a bookcase. "I can't believe my mom put this under *The* instead of *Snowman.* Let me put this puppy in, and then I'll get my fishing pole."

So much for impressing Andy with her things. In fact, nothing about her seemed to impress him at all. Was that the reason she found herself caring what he thought of her?

Now, as the outside air chilled her skin, she wondered why she was even doing this stupid trick. They'd sneaked out without their coats, and she was beginning to freeze. She rubbed the end of her nose with the palm of her hand. It was numb. Great, she muttered to herself. Now I'll get frostbite on my nose. Perfect.

Andy's dark shape appeared in front of her. "I've hooked the line into the screen," he whispered. "They're still talking. Do you have the bow?"

"It's right here." She held up the violin bow.

"Okay, let's reel this out a little further. We can hide behind that tree. Even if they look, they'll never be able to see us." He chuckled a low, menacing chuckle.

"Valdez, I do believe you're enjoying this."

Holding the rod out in front of him, Andy slowly backed up. He stopped in front of a fir tree twenty feet from the window.

"Come on, Haley!"

Haley scrambled over and crouched next to him. Through the window, she could see her parents sipping coffee.

Andy pulled the line tight. There was enough light from the window for Haley to see his hair ruffle in the chilly breeze. His eyelashes were so thick they cast a shadow on his cheek. He leaned close and Haley could feel his breath.

"Go!" he commanded.

Just as she had on "Family Love," Haley dragged the bow across the fishing line as if she were playing a one-stringed violin. Andy's eyes stayed glued to the window. If the trick worked the way it should, the whole dining room would be filled with an eerie moaning sound. Nothing. She gave it a longer, harder play. Through the window, Haley watched as Rita poured another cup of coffee. Her father threw back his head in laughter, and her mother took a dainty bite of cake.

"Go faster," he ordered.

With short, rapid motions, Haley began to saw on the fishing line.

Once, Michael looked at the window, then went back to his coffee. No one else even flinched.

"I don't get it," Andy told her. "Here, you hold the pole, I'll try the bow."

"Did you get the hook all the way in?" Haley asked.

"Of course I did. Now, keep it steady, and pull the line way tight." The pole almost flew out of her hands when Andy began to saw on the line. From where they sat, it sounded like scritching scratching noises, but nothing more.

"It's supposed to be loud," Andy said. "When you did it on the set, was it loud?"

"That was a couple of years ago. Let me think. I put the hook in and . . . Wait a minute. Shoot! I think I know what the problem is."

"What?"

Shaking her head, Haley said, "The loud moaning stuff was from the sound-effects man. It wasn't real. I can't believe I didn't think of that!"

Andy slumped into the grass. He let the bow dangle limp from his fingertips.

"All kinds of sounds are dubbed into the tape. Sometimes, even the lines we say are recorded separately and added later. Sorry."

"Oh, well," Andy said. "What I want to know is, why would they have something on TV that doesn't work? I mean, doesn't anybody check out that kind of stuff?"

"It's only a television show." Haley's teeth began to chatter. Andy didn't seem cold at all.

"We better get back in before you freeze to death. I'll unhook the line. Here, you hold the bow again."

This time, Andy walked right up to the window and unhooked the line. No one inside even noticed.

Later, inside, Haley pulled the quilt around her tightly. *The Snowman* flickered across the screen, but Andy wasn't watching it, either. He sat at the edge of the sofa, pulling on one thumb, then the other. She could tell he was going over and over the trick in his mind, trying to figure it out.

He snapped his fingers. Haley jumped.

"I've got it. Our screens aren't aluminum. I bet that trick would have been slick if the screens were aluminum instead of nylon. That's got to be the reason! You know, I couldn't see some writer putting that in your show if it didn't work."

"Andy—give it a rest. This is not a big deal. Why do you even care?"

"It just bugs me. I don't like to believe something is real and then find out later that it isn't." He let his hands dangle between his knees.

"That's the exact opposite of me. I mean, if you think about it, everything I've done has been fake. I guess I like that better than dealing with real stuff."

He looked at her with genuine curiosity. "Why?"

Shrugging, Haley said, "I don't know. Because." She looked off over his head. No one had ever asked her how she felt about acting, and she wasn't quite sure how to put it into words. The world of "Family Love," or even commercials, was the world she felt comfortable in. And now Andy, with his dark eyes that seemed to stare right inside of her, was asking her to explain it. "Because, when I'm acting, it's really . . . safe."

"Safe? How is acting safe? You're in front of a million people with a camera right in your face." Shaking his head, he said, "I don't get what you're saying."

"You've never been an actor, I mean in a school play or anything, right?"

"Nope."

"It's kind of hard to explain." She took a deep breath and blew it through her lips. "Well, for one thing, with a script, I know how things are going to turn out from the very beginning. It's like, I can flip to the end, and there it is. And every problem, no matter what it is, always gets solved in twenty-two minutes, guaranteed. But it just doesn't work like that in real life."

"I guess. But at least whatever happens in real life is true."

"I know it is, but still ..." she let the last word dangle. The movie music swelled, and the credits began to roll. That meant it was about nine o'clock, and her parents would be ready to leave. With a flash of surprise, Haley realized that she didn't want to go. Andy was asking what she, Haley Loring, thought, instead of waiting to be entertained by Samantha Love. It felt good.

"Haley, I wanted to ask you—"

Just then, the sound of her mother's voice floated down the hallway. "Ha-leeey."

"Okay," she called back, "I'm coming."

Turning back to Andy, she said, "So what did you want to ask me?"

Andy shook his head. "Forget it. Your folks are waiting."

Unfolding herself from the chair, she stretched her arms.

"Come on, Haley! You've got school in the morning."

"Well, I guess it's time to go. Thanks a lot, Andy. This was fun."

He smiled at her. "Even if the fishing pole thing was a complete dud?"

"Hey, at least we tried. See you tomorrow."

"Yeah. See ya."

A fine mist of rain had just begun to come down. Haley climbed in the back while her parents slipped into the front seat of their car. Her father started the engine. The windshield wipers squeaked back and forth across the glass, and the light of an oncoming car made their faces shine gray.

"I had a great time," her mother began. "Did you?"

"Wonderful. They're terrific people." Her father cleared his throat. "By the way, Jane. When we were having coffee, did you hear anything . . . odd?"

"You mean that thing that sounded like a dying cat? Yes!" She grabbed his forearm. "I thought it was just me!"

"At first I thought it might be the plumbing."

"So did I. But it came from outside."

"I kept expecting the table to rise up from under us!"

"I thought maybe a ghost would appear! Nobody said a thing, so I just pretended not to hear. I still have goose bumps.

"What's so funny?" her mother demanded. "Haley, what is so funny? You're snorting back there like a pig."

"Nothing." It took all of her acting skills to keep from laughing out loud. She couldn't wait for tomorrow to come, so she could tell Andy the whole story. Their trick had worked!

The rainstorm from the night before had turned to snow and then blown on, leaving the sky a clear blue and the ground a dazzling white. Outside the school, kindergartners lined up in boots and fuzzy mittens. Little pointed hats had been tied with bows underneath their pink chins. But the sixth graders from Haley's class left their coats wide open and stomped through the slush in sneakers as if they were immune to the cold. With her back against the brick wall, she kept scanning the crowd for Andy. Where was he? School would start in less than five minutes, and he still wasn't there.

"Hey, Haley. How do you like the blizzard?" Andy called through cupped hands. He was right at the point where the road met the sidewalk that led to the school. He must have been looking for her, too.

"You think you cut it close enough, Valdez?" Haley called back. "The bell's going to ring any second."

His backpack was slung over one shoulder, and he ran quickly through the snow to where Haley stood.

Was it the reflection from the snow, or were his eyes extra bright? He leaned into the wall, panting.

"I almost didn't recognize you. You've only got about an inch of your face showing."

"I want the beach. Give me the beach!" Haley chattered. Her brown bomber jacket was zipped as far as it could go, and even though there wasn't another girl around who wore one, Haley had a red cashmere hat yanked down to her eyelids. Her matching cashmere gloves were on her hands, which were tucked up under her armpits.

"This is nothing. Wait until January." Andy laughed. His teeth were white.

Haley felt suddenly shy. After a few beats of silence, she grabbed his wrist and said, "Oh, guess what? My folks heard the noise last night and about freaked out! It worked! They think your house is haunted."

"Fantastic! That's great." With a nervous motion, Andy pulled his zipper tab up and down. His eyes went to the front of the building, then to Haley. "I've got something for you." He jerked his backpack off his shoulder and unzipped it. From inside he produced a legal-sized envelope and stuffed it into her hand. "Here," he said simply.

With her teeth, Haley yanked off her glove. She slit open the envelope and removed a handmade card. It said,

> *"This is the chance*
> *For a Halloween Dance*
> *That, I promise you, won't be the same,*
> *If you will just look*
> *At the end of the hook,*
> *You'll see that I fished out your name."*

A fish hook had been glued onto the paper, and a line had been drawn that wound around to a sketched fishing pole. Dripping from the hook, in the shape of a fish, was the name "Haley."

"It's stupid. I don't know—Ms. Walter said to be original. I filed the points down on the hook so you wouldn't cut yourself. It's the one we used last night. I thought it might be like a souvenir or something."

"I love it!"

"The dance is only a week and two days from now, and we've got to do costumes, so I thought, maybe today we could get together and work on them. We can go right after school, if you want."

"Sure. Great!"

Relieved, Andy broke into a wide smile. She smiled back. For the first time that morning, Haley felt warm.

It had taken Haley a moment to get back into her Samantha Love character, probably because she'd been out of it since the night before. Head back, shoulders straight, Haley slipped into her seat and into Samantha Love. When lunchtime came, she and all the other girls from her class squeezed once again around the lunch table. Eleven of them had sack lunches, and eight of those contained yogurt. None of them had gone for the tofu.

"Are you having cucumber sticks again?" Mindy asked her.

"Yeah, I eat them every day. I'm a creature of habit." Studying her cucumber stick, Haley added, "All the bad ones, of course."

Everyone at the table laughed. "You are so FUNNY," Cherry told her. "Oh, speaking of funny, get this. Bruce

74

came over last night. He wrote, 'Will you go with me to the Halloween Dance?' on a piece of paper and put it in a pink balloon. I hate pink.''

"Kyle asked me," a girl in a blue sweater said. "But all he did was go, 'I got your name,' and I said, 'Okay.' "

"All those who have NOT been asked to the Halloween dance yet, raise your hands!" Cherry commanded.

Two hands went up in the air.

"Wait a minute! Haley, where's your hand? Did you get asked? When?" Cherry demanded.

Trying to sound nonchalant, she answered, "This morning."

"By who?" Mindy looked at her in amazement. "I can't believe you didn't say something before this. Who asked you? Was it Ron?"

"No."

"Eric?"

"Nope."

"Brandon? Kenneth?"

Haley shook her head. This was a moment she'd been half dreading, because Andy wasn't exactly popular. Samantha Love would have been mad about drawing Andy, but Haley Loring thought it was just fine.

"Well! Tell us!" The table leaned forward excitedly.

"Andy Valdez." And then, just like Samantha Love would have done, she shrugged and added, "What-a-ya-gonna-do?"

"You've got to be kidding," Cherry giggled. "Your luck is even worse than mine. How'd he ask you?"

"He made a kind of poem thing."

Cherry made a face. "A poem? A POEM? Give me a break! Where is it? Let me see!"

A wave of "This ought to be good" and "I would have guessed that Andy Valdez would write a poem" rippled up the table.

Swallowing, Haley said, "I don't want to go and get it. I mean, I'm eating, and it's in my desk. Anyway, that's who I'm going with. Andy Valdez." She began to play with the creases in her brown lunch bag. But for some reason, Cherry wouldn't drop it.

"I have got to see this note. He is such a geek—I bet it's just the worst! Did it rhyme? Knowing Andy, I bet it did. He'll probably turn it in for extra credit."

Haley kept her eyes on the bag. One fold, then another, then another, until she'd made a paper fan. "He's not that bad," she murmured.

"Not that bad? Not that bad!?!" Cherry cried. "Haley, you haven't been in Garland long enough to understand who Andy Valdez is. He's a curve buster. The grades in the whole class go down because he doesn't have a thing to do but study. Plus"—Cherry was getting heated now—"PLUS, he is the teacher's pet of the century."

Mindy narrowed her eyes. "Last year, he played the violin for our Christmas program in a red velvet bow tie!"

"He turned in his term report a whole month early," Grace told her. "Can you believe it? No one turns in stuff early."

"You don't get it 'cause you're new," Cherry explained. She rested her hand—the nails had been painted with lavender fingernail polish—against Haley's shoulder. "Believe me, if you got Andy Valdez, then you'd better catch that flu you told me about. Trust me."

The girls at the table nodded in agreement. Haley felt

as if she were shrinking inside herself. Part of her wanted to stand up for Andy, but an even bigger part was afraid of losing the only fans she had left. What would Samantha do? Pulling her hair into a ponytail, she twisted it into a bun, then let it drop in a smooth fall of waves down her back. Whatever she said, it was important that she look as though nothing bothered her. "Well, of course I don't want to go with him, but his mom and mine are friends. I'm stuck."

Cherry had on an oversized purple knit sweater. She pushed the sleeves up past her elbows as she spoke. "I thought you said your parents would let you get out of it."

"Well, they usually would let me do whatever I want, but my mom and Andy's mother are super close. I'm going as a favor to my mom."

Nodding in agreement, Cherry said, "I know what you mean about having to go 'cause of your mother. My mom says I have to be nice, even though it's Bruce."

"Mine, too." Grace shuddered. "I got Vincent. His hands sweat and he spits when he talks. Yuck!"

"Well," Haley said, shrugging her shoulders, "I guess that's just the way it goes."

"Yeah," everyone at the table agreed. "I guess."

Haley breathed a little sigh of relief. She would go to the dance, and all the girls still believed in Samantha.

The cafeteria jangled with noise. Trays banged against tables, benches screeched across the linoleum floor, voices, laughter, all mixed into a clamor.

Mindy sipped her milk. Cherry played with her yogurt, scraping the insides with a spoon. Suddenly, her face cleared. "Wait a minute!" she squealed. "I just

77

thought of something. Haley, you don't want to go to the dance, right?''

"Um, no," Haley answered.

"Okay, I don't want to go, and Grace doesn't want to go either."

"No kidding," Grace said. "Somebody, please, get me out of it!"

"So"—Cherry knit her fingers together and pointed her knuckles at Grace and Haley—"the three of us could get the pretend flu together." She looked at Haley intently. "I mean, I might not be able to pull the flu off, but you could. You're such a good actress that everybody would trust that you were for real."

"That's a radical idea," Grace breathed.

"Mrs. Walter would believe Haley. Then she'd accept it if we said we had it, too."

Grace nodded excitedly. "It could be like a twenty-four-hour thing, and we could all get well by the next day so we wouldn't miss the real Halloween. I love it."

"That is so perfect!" Mindy squealed. "I've been feeling so bad about you guys, 'cause I got Chase and all. But you could stay home and call each other on the phone and everything!"

What should she do? What could she do? Everything was getting planned and settled while she sat there like a stone. Feelings of panic welled inside her. These girls liked her, of that she was certain, but she hadn't been there very long. She needed to be careful, or they wouldn't see Samantha Love; she'd be Haley Loring, loser. Time. She needed to buy time until she could figure out exactly what she should do. She could always say yes right now and then change her mind.

"You haven't said a word, Haley," Cherry prompted. "What do you think?"

Thirteen oval faces, twenty-six round eyes, focused on her.

"I'm in," Haley told them. "No problem."

"All right, class, listen up," Mrs. Walter announced. "The dance is next Friday, and that gives you a little over a week to work on your costumes. Now remember, this is teamwork."

Mindy flashed Chase a brilliant smile.

"You've got to work together." Mrs. Walter began to pace the front of the room. Today, she had on a green sweatshirt. Snaking down her back was a long braid that ended in a black-and-green ribbon. A black cat with emerald eyes had been painted on the front of her sweatshirt with fabric glitter, and as she walked, her braid swished back and forth like the cat's twitchy tail.

"The idea is NOT to spend a lot of money on outfits. I don't want your parents to think they have to shell out cash just for this dance. Be creative. Be original!"

"Be quiet," Cherry muttered.

Andy looked over his shoulder at Haley. He'd returned to his seat up front, and Haley could watch the back of his head during class. With his fingers slightly cupped, Andy gave her a small wave. From the corner of her eye, Haley checked to see if Cherry was looking. She wasn't. Haley gave a tiny wave back.

"Is there anything else you need to know?" Mrs. Walter asked.

Mindy raised her hand. "Can we wear masks?"

"Good question. I would prefer you didn't, just because visibility can be bad. But if you think you really have to wear one, then put it on at the dance and take it off when you leave. Fair enough? Okay! Anything else? Grace?"

"You said we're being graded on this, right?"

Mrs. Walter nodded.

"So what if one of us gets really, truly sick? Are we going to fail?"

Sighing, Mrs. Walter said, "Of course not. But please, people, wash your hands, get plenty of sleep, and drink orange juice. This is going to be a very fun night. Okay, let's move on. Math books, chapter seven, page eighty-three."

As the lids to the desks shot up, a note landed on Haley's lap. It said, "This costume thing is a bummer. I don't want to waste my time 'cause I'm NOT going, and I KNOW it's the same for you! What do you think?"

Haley grabbed her pencil and scribbled, "We can put our arms and legs through grocery sacks and say we're going to go as bag ladies. Simple, fast, cheap. Tee hee." She tossed the note over on Cherry's desk. When Cherry read it, she giggled and mouthed, "I love it!"

Opening her math book, Haley tried to concentrate on the numbers, but they seemed to wriggle across the page like tiny numerical bugs. What was she going to do? How had she gotten herself into this mess? Andy would be meeting her after school, and then what?

Maybe she should go with him and work on a real simple costume, one that wouldn't be a big deal if she decided to skip the dance. She looked at the back of Andy's head, at the sharp line his hair made when it skimmed the collar of his shirt. No, he was definitely the type to give one hundred percent to making a costume. He'd probably want to go as Lieutenant Worf on "Star Trek: The Next Generation."

Maybe she should tell him that she was busy today, she'd call him, and they'd do lunch sometime. That's what everyone in Hollywood did when they were trying to buy time. But the truth was—she wanted to see him. She liked being with him, liked watching the way his cheeks crinkled at the edges when he smiled. Frowning, Haley dug her fingernails into her palms as she tried to weigh the choices. She really liked Andy, but the other girls didn't, and she needed them, too. Maybe—

"Haley? Ms. Loring, are you with us?" Mrs. Walter's voice broke into her thoughts. "What's the answer to number four?"

"Um . . ." she glanced at the problem. She could feel her cheeks burn.

"Well?"

"Let's see," Haley faltered.

"One hundred and forty-six," Andy declared. He flashed Haley a smile.

"That's correct . . . HALEY," Mrs. Walter said, looking directly at Andy. "All right, class, let's all pay attention to our math now. No more daydreaming."

"What a dweeb," Cherry muttered. "He always has to show off how smart he is."

Staring at her book, Haley said nothing.

The rest of the afternoon, she tried her best to avoid

Andy. When he passed out test papers, she didn't meet his eyes, but pretended instead to search underneath her desk for a pencil. She watched Andy's crisp white sneakers hesitate, then move down the aisle before she dared to look up. At recess, she hung against the wall, surrounded by Cherry and the others. Once Andy approached her with a kickball in his hands. As he came closer, she'd grabbed onto Grace's arm and laughed hard, just the way Samantha Love always laughed. When she'd looked back in Andy's direction, he was walking the other way, bouncing the ball against the asphalt in time with his step. He's going to notice that you're avoiding him, Haley scolded herself. How long do you think you can keep this up? She'd slumped into the wall, feeling the rough nap of the brick against her palms.

When the last bell rang, Cherry was at her elbow, shadowing Haley as she made her way toward the door.

"Hey, I was thinking, do you want to get together at my house?" Cherry asked.

"Sorry," Haley said, shaking her head. "I'm booked solid for the rest of the day. Gotta run now, bye."

Grabbing her knapsack and her coat, Haley ran into the rest room, where she splashed her face with cold water and wiped it with a rough paper towel. Noises from the hallway echoed off the tile walls as she waited for the crowd of kids to thin, then disappear.

She knew what she was doing was sneaky and low. "You are such a jerk," she yelled to her reflection in the mirror. "Just tell them you like Andy. Just TELL them." But fear rose up inside as her other voice whispered, "Then they'll know you're a fake. They'll know you're not Samantha. You'll be dumped, just like Sheena dumped you. You won't have anyone.''

Breathing deeply, she tried to get control. Finally, she crumpled up the paper towel and threw it into a trash can.

It was quiet in the hallway. No one was there. She'd only been in the rest room ten minutes, but it seemed as if the entire school had vanished.

"Haley, what are you hanging around here for?" Mrs. Walter asked. "Usually the students can't wait to get outside."

"I—I was washing my hands."

"Well, good for you. Proper hygiene is a wonderful thing. See you tomorrow."

"Bye, Mrs. Walter," Haley said.

A few boys from the lower grades were busy picking up the bright orange cones that had been set out to mark the crosswalks. Two girls were lowering the flag, but she didn't know either one of them.

"Haley," a voice cried. "Over here!"

Leaning against the wall, in the exact spot where he'd been that morning, stood Andy. The collar of his navy jacket had been pulled up, and his backpack lay crumpled at his feet. Haley scanned the schoolyard. Almost everyone had already gone, so she smiled and waved back.

"I've been waiting for you. I almost gave up."

"I'm here now," she answered.

"Good. I wanted to get to work on the costumes. I made up a list of some suggestions. What do you think of these?"

Grabbing the piece of paper, Haley read:

Dracula and a girl with a bite mark on her neck
Frankenstein and the Bride of Frankenstein
Monsters
Headless people

"You don't like them," Andy said. "I can tell by your face."

"I don't know," Haley protested. "I think this list needs some work."

"Okay, fine. You tell me YOUR ideas."

"Give me a minute. The headless people thing has some possibilities!"

Haley realized once again how much she liked being with him. He didn't seem to mind the way she'd avoided him. In fact, he probably hadn't even noticed. It was possible that she could keep her distance from Andy at school, and then be friends with him the rest of the time. She could be Samantha Love by day and Haley Loring after school. As for going to the dance, well, she really didn't need to make a decision about it right that minute. There was no hurry. She just needed to keep both sides of her life separate. It was a risky plan, but it just might work.

Five days later, the sun cast weak shadows across the sidewalk in front of the school. The morning snow had already melted, leaving jeweled beads of water on the tips of the grass. Across the street grew three wild apple trees; underneath them lay a thick blanket of red apples. She breathed in the faint smell of applesauce.

"It's a miracle! You're here!" Andy yelled.

They hurried toward each other, Andy walking faster than Haley. When they met near the middle of the schoolyard, he asked, "Where were you? You promised you'd be on time today."

"Sorry, I got held up," she lied.

"But you're always late! Every day."

"Sorry. I'm just slow."

The truth was that she'd been hiding in the rest room again, like she had every afternoon during the past week. After the last bell, she'd grab her coat and sprint out of the classroom and run straight into the girls' room, concealing herself in the very last blue-and-white-tiled stall. As soon as all the noise died down, she'd carefully open the door, creep down the empty hallway and out to the schoolyard where Andy would be waiting. So far, it had worked fine.

"Does your mom care that we're always going to your house after school? I feel bad because I'm eating all your food."

Shrugging, Haley said, "Trust me, my mom loves to feed people. You're making her very happy."

"Yeah, my mom likes to do the food thing, too. It's just—she's gone until six."

"I'd hate that. My mom loves being at home with me, and I like having her there."

"That's good," Andy murmured.

They fell into step side by side. Haley felt the cold air chill her lungs, and when she breathed out she saw little puffs of steam. Andy rubbed the top of his head with his hand. He looked down at her and said, "Of course, I'm really stretching a point when I call that healthy stuff food. Leaves and twigs, that's what you Loring people eat."

"Today we'll be serving you bran flakes with a sea-weed twist." Placing her fingertips to her lips, she kissed them just like a chef would. "It's mah-ve-lous, darling. Très Hollywood."

"Don't you ever eat chocolate?"

"Nope. Too fattening. Besides, if you eat healthy, you'll live longer."

"No, I won't," Andy said, grinning. "It'll just feel that way."

She knew he was teasing. He joked with her a lot, and she loved it. Whenever the nagging feeling about the dance crept over her, she shoved it down into a deep place where she didn't look. Worry about it tomorrow, she told herself. But her tomorrows were running out.

A cluster of evergreen trees stood guard in front of a home. The trees had been trimmed into huge triangles, with the largest tree hovering over the smaller ones. It reminded Haley of a mother gathering her children into a green velvet skirt.

"Do you ever look at clouds or something and see dolphins or camels?" she asked Andy. As soon as the words slipped out of her mouth, she was sorry. What a lame thing to say, right out loud! Cherry would have laughed at her for sure, but Andy didn't even flinch.

"I don't know. I guess. Sometimes." He peered into the sky. "Except right now I don't see anything."

"No—I mean, like, do you look at a house and see a face? Like that one over there?" She pointed to a home with two framed windows over a brown garage door. "Doesn't that look like a face to you?"

"Sort of." And then, "Yeah, I see it. I've never thought a house looked like anything but a house before." He squinted at her. "Is this some sort of acting thing?"

87

"No, it's just me."

The next home had a string of three-inch pumpkin lights wound around an outdoor railing. Pasted on the window were pictures of white ghosts, with *Oooooooo*'s coming out of their mouths. With a sweep of his hand, Andy said, "Look at that house there. I see pumpkins. And ghosts. Lots and lots of pumpkins and ghosts."

Punching his arm, Haley said, "Shut up, Valdez." But they both laughed.

Suddenly, Andy's face changed expression. "Listen, we've GOT to decide on the costumes. The dance is in two days, and all we've done is come up with what we're NOT going to be. Have you got any new ideas?"

A prickly feeling pinched her. So far, she'd been acting like she was going to go, but stalling on making costumes. Should she keep on pretending? Could she? Haley clenched her fists to squeeze away the prickles. She was an actress. She could handle this.

"Well, I don't know if you've ever seen Andrew Lloyd Webber's *Cats,*" she began. "You know, the play? I was thinking—"

"Thinking. That's good. A first step."

"Ha ha. Okay, how about if the two of us go as cats? I could do the makeup because I know how. I even have some fake beard stuff I could glue on."

Snorting, Andy said, "You're real funny. I thought maybe cowboys. Do you have any Western stuff?"

"Wait a minute!" Haley exclaimed. They were right in front of her house as she stopped and looked at him. "I wasn't kidding about the *Cats* thing. It would be different! I mean, a cowboy? Get serious." She began to saunter as if her legs were bowed from years in the saddle. Chewing an imaginary blade of grass, she hitched up her jeans and drawled, "Howdy, partner. Got any of them thar beans?"

"I suppose you think this would be better?" Andy jumped and pirouetted like a cat caught in a blender. He was so spastic, his backpack flew off and landed in a nearby bush.

"Pul-eeze." Haley laughed.

"Listen, if I came dancing into Garland in a cat costume, even Bruce wouldn't talk to me anymore. I mean, face it. The whole class already thinks I'm weird enough." He fished the backpack out of the branches and slipped it on. "Coming to school as a cat would be the end."

The statement caught Haley by surprise. She knew what the other kids thought of Andy, but for some reason she'd assumed he was completely in the dark about it. It made her feel strange to hear him admit it like that. She looked at her shoes and then squinted at her house. The inside lights cast a warm glow.

"Well, anyway, I'm hungry. Let's go inside."

"Maybe your mother will serve us saucers of milk."

Shaking her head, Haley said, "Nope. Definitely beans. Weenies and beans, that's what me 'n' the cowboys like."

Sprinting up the stairs, Haley threw open the door. "I'm home, Mom! I brought Andy with me! Mom. Mom?"

"Honey, just a second, I'm in the middle of something." Her mother's voice floated down from upstairs.

"Okay, but hurry. We're hungry! Let's wait in the kitchen," Haley told Andy. "Mom said she was going to make some natural whole-grain fruit bars today, and they're my favorites."

After they'd made their way to the kitchen, Andy

dropped his backpack on the floor and plunked himself into a maple chair. With anyone else, Haley would have been embarrassed by the difference in the way their houses looked. Even though the Loring kitchen was clean, the teakettle wallpaper had yellowed, and their countertop had blisters on it. But she knew it wouldn't matter to Andy.

"Don't you ever eat anything that doesn't sound like it came from the health-food store?" Andy asked.

"No way. If I don't watch my figure, then no one will."

His face curled into an elfin grin. "You ought to try some chocolate chocolate cookies. It'd be good for you. In fact"—he let his fist slap the tabletop—I'll bring some tomorrow."

"No! If you bring chocolate, I'll eat it, and pretty soon I'd end up looking like Wilbur. All stuffed and round."

"Wait a minute!" Andy jumped from his chair and walked over to where Haley stood. He looked down, right into her eyes. The wind had ruffed up the edge of his hair, and the light from behind created a dark fringe around his head. "Hey," he said. "I've got it! I know what we can be for the dance."

"What?" She hadn't realized he was so tall.

"This is the greatest idea! We could go as Wilbur! Both of us. My dad has a couple of pairs of bib overalls—"

"We could stuff them with newspapers and wear hats and gloves—"

"And maybe we could walk behind Mrs. Walter and scare the spit out of her—"

" 'Cause we'll look exactly like her Wilbur. I like it! Valdez, you're a genius!"

Right then, Haley didn't care about Cherry. She didn't care about Grace or Mindy or anyone. She knew that no matter what, no matter who got mad at her or what they said, she was going to that dance. With Andy. The only real friend she had.

The doorbell rang.

"Mom, could you get that?" Haley cried. "Andy and I are busy in the kitchen."

"Sure, honey," her mother called back.

From his seat at the kitchen table, Andy said, "My mom always makes me get the door. You've sure got your mom trained."

"Well, I KNOW it's for her. No one ever comes to see ME. Besides"—Haley gave a little bow—"it wouldn't be polite to keep you waiting for your refreshment, now, would it?"

"Of course not." Andy grinned. In a terrible British accent, he added, "By all means, carry on."

Haley returned to her job of finding something good to drink from the refrigerator. She glanced up at the brass wall clock overhead. Four thirty-six. That meant just another hour with Andy, and then he'd have to go. She didn't want him to leave. She and Andy hadn't done much but munch on food and plan their Wilbur costumes, but it had been fun. Andy's red-white-and-black sweatshirt had the words CHICAGO BULLS printed across it, so she'd spent half the time teasing him about backing the wrong team. "You should root for the Lakers!" she'd insisted. "Purple and gold—those are the right colors."

"I only go with winners," Andy had retorted.

"Ha. Then you're really in trouble. The Bulls are pitiful." She clucked her tongue and added, "Really pitiful."

"I bet you only root for the Lakers because purple is your favorite color. Am I right?"

Haley had leaned across the table, resting her weight on her knuckles. Narrowing her eyes, she'd told him, "That is such a guy thing to say. I picked the Lakers because they're the best."

"What about purple? Is that your favorite color?"

"Nope. It's red." And then she'd stopped in surprise. "No, wait a minute. That's Samantha Love's favorite color. Mine is . . ."

The spectrum of colors had flashed through her mind. Robin's-egg blue, seashell pink, and soft greens. She wasn't sure what she, Haley Loring, liked best. "I think my favorite color is . . . yellow." She'd looked at Andy.

"Mine's blue. So there goes the theory. But the Bulls still are the best."

"Bull," Haley had laughed.

And now the afternoon was almost gone. From down the hallway, she could hear her mother opening the front door. If only she could keep Andy in the kitchen a while longer. With him, she could be Haley Loring. She could be herself.

"Haley, you've got another friend here. His name is Bruce, and he says he needs to see Andy."

Great, Haley groaned. There was hardly any time left, and now she had to share it with Bruce. Bruce and his pasty freckles. She could feel herself cringe.

Andy looked up at Haley. "Bruce is here? I wonder what he wants?"

"You got me!" Haley shrugged.

The voices of her mom and Bruce echoed down the hallway. "Go straight ahead," her mother instructed. "Haley and Andy are in the kitchen. Make sure you get a fruit bar."

"Um, okay," Bruce replied.

Haley could hear Bruce before she could see him: clomp, clomp, clomp. She heard a pause, and then the clomping faded away. He'd made a wrong turn into the family room.

"BRUCE—" Haley shouted, "we're down here. In the KITCHEN!"

The clomping started again. Moments later Bruce appeared at the doorway.

One look at his feet and Haley could tell why his footsteps thumped. He'd worn a pair of blue snowboots to school, and he still had them on. His brown pants had a frayed spot in the knee. Although his black coat showed a pop-eyed, drooling, skateboard-riding monster embroidered across the front, it didn't help. Bruce, Haley decided, was hopeless.

"Um, hi, Haley. Is Andy there? I mean here?"

With her finger, Haley pointed to where Andy sat.

"Oh, hi, Andy. I didn't see you." Bruce gave a laugh that sounded something like a snort.

"Hey, Bruce. What for can I do ya?" Andy asked. He seemed genuinely pleased that Bruce had come over, which annoyed Haley. Her plan was to get rid of Bruce

94

fast. She didn't need Andy encouraging him to hang around.

"I, um, needed to talk to you about the dance. You said you and Haley were going to get together after school today, and I tried your house and no one answered so I came over here. Is that okay?"

"Sure. Have a sit." Andy motioned to a chair. "Have a fruit bar. They're really pretty good. What's up?'

Bruce dropped into a chair beside Andy. Haley stayed rooted beside the refrigerator. What was the deal here? Andy was giving directions as if it were HIS kitchen instead of hers. And she hadn't wanted Bruce to actually sit down. Maybe he wouldn't get up again.

"Boy, those fruity things look great. Did you cook them?" Bruce asked Haley.

"No. My mother BAKED them. What did you need to know about the dance?"

Instead of answering, Bruce took a large bite of fruit bar. When he chewed, it looked as if he were chomping on a wad of clay.

Chew, chew, chew, then swallow. Haley tapped her fingers against the countertop. Samantha Love would know how to get Bruce out of her house. She'd hurry him right along. "The dance, Bruce," she said pointedly. "The DANCE. What did you need to know?"

"Um, I don't think Cherry wants to go with me."

Big surprise, Haley thought. She crossed her arms.

Andy looked genuinely concerned. "What makes you think that?" he asked.

"Well, lots of things," Bruce said, pausing after every word. "Every time I call Cherry, she says she can't talk because she's washing her cat. I don't think she even has a cat. And when I try to talk to her at

95

school, she just walks away. We don't have our costumes or anything."

"Don't worry about it. Haley and I just decided on ours this afternoon. Maybe you just caught Cherry at a bad time," Andy offered.

Maybe it's because you talk so s-low-ly, Haley thought. Watching him, it seemed as if Bruce had to visualize every word, turn it over in his mind, run it from his brain to his mouth, and then move his lips. She would have preferred to hear fingernails squeak across a chalkboard.

Bruce took another bite.

Pul-eeze, Haley screamed in her mind. Don't eat anymore. Talk!

"Are you thirsty?" Andy asked him.

When Bruce nodded, Andy said, "Haley, could you get Bruce some milk?"

Gritting her teeth, Haley grunted, "Sure. Love to. My pleasure." She went to the cupboard, grabbed a glass, took it to the refrigerator, filled it, then set it in front of Bruce with a bang. He was still chewing. Finally, he swallowed a big, gulping swallow. He took a swig of milk and wiped his mouth with the back of his hand.

"So, Bruce, you were saying about the DANCE ... Remember? That's why you came over?"

"Oh, yeah. Okay, every time I make a suggestion, Cherry goes, 'Whatever.' I said, 'Cherry, do you want to go to the dance dressed up like Elvis Presley?' And she goes, 'Whatever.' Then I said, 'Well, would you rather go like Batman and Catwoman?' And she goes, 'Whatever.' And then she starts to cough like she's really sick."

"Maybe she's got some allergies," Andy said.

Darn right. She's allergic to you, Haley added silently.

Andy rested his chin on his hand. "So, how can I help?"

"Well, I had this plan. I thought maybe we could all go to the dance together. You, me, and Cherry and Haley."

"Hey, that's a great idea, Bruce," Andy said. "Don't you think that's a great idea, Haley?"

"Whatever."

Andy shot her a look, but Bruce didn't seem to notice. He took another bite and continued talking. Little crumbs of food sprinkled onto the tabletop as he spoke.

"You guys are my only hope. You know what I heard today? I heard that Cherry's planning on faking the flu so she for sure won't have to go with me."

Haley drew in a sharp breath. Cold fingers gripped her insides. Their plan had leaked out! Even though every girl had sworn not to tell, it hadn't been a secret for even a week.

"What's the matter, Haley?" Andy asked. "You look kind of white."

"Nothing's wrong. You know, Bruce, you can't believe everything you hear."

With his eyes glued to Haley, Andy asked Bruce, "Who told you about this flu thing?"

"Let's see. Mindy is friends with Sandra, and she told Sandra all about it, and Sandra is my sister Laura's friend, and Laura told me. I believe it." Rubbing his nose with his knuckle, Bruce added, "There are two other girls who aren't going to go 'cause they hate the guys they're stuck with. None of them will work on their costumes, either. They don't want to waste their time when they're not going. I think one of the girls is Grace."

"Is that true, Haley?"

Shrugging, Haley said, "How should I know?" But her voice came out in a squeak. That hadn't happened before. Usually she was pretty good at acting. But with Andy's dark eyes boring into her, she felt off balance. "Would you like some milk, too?" she asked Andy.

"No."

Smiling brilliantly, Haley said, "Okay! Well, I'll just put this stuff away."

Like a lion watching its prey, Andy never moved his eyes from Haley for an instant. She could feel the edges of her ears burn.

Patting his stomach, Bruce pushed himself away from the table and stood. "Well, guys, I gotta go. Thanks for the food, Haley. I'm glad we're all going together. See ya, Andy."

"See you later, Bruce."

As Bruce clumped away, Haley pretended to study the violets that her mother had brought from California. Their petals were as dark and velvety as an insect's wing. Next to them sat a vase with lemon-yellow carnations that smelled like hard candy, and next to that, a small pot contained white mums with peppermint stripes. Her finger drifted from the ragged edge of the carnation to the soft, fuzzy lip of the violet to the mum's feathery petals. But she really didn't see the blossoms. All she could feel were those eyes of Andy's. They drilled into her, reading her mind, dissecting her thoughts. He knew that she and Cherry hung around together. She'd been stalling on the costumes all week. He might have guessed that she was going to be one of the Halloween flu victims. This could definitely be a problem. Andy was pretty smart, but she'd have to be smarter. After all, she was the actress.

"So! Let's finish the list for our Wilbur costumes," Haley chirped. "Do you have any burlap? You know, like to make a mask or something . . ." When she looked at his face, her sentence trailed away.

"Are you going to catch the flu on Friday?" Andy's voice was deadly. "I want to know now."

"No! No way!" Even though she commanded her eyes to stare at him, her gaze dropped to the floor. Why couldn't she pull it off when it came to Andy? It was as if he knew her better than anyone.

"Okay," she said, toeing the floor with the tip of her Nike. "Maybe we talked about the POSSIBILITY of getting sick. But I changed my mind already. I swear I did. I want to go."

"But you and Cherry and Grace planned to get out of it." It wasn't a question. It was a statement of fact. Haley didn't see much use in arguing, so she nodded. Now he knew the worst. She'd come clean. Everything would be okay.

Andy frowned so deeply that his eyebrows knit together. His jaw twitched the way it had the first day they'd met. "I can't believe you guys planned on standing us up. Jeez, Haley, I thought we were friends."

"We are—"

"Oh, right. Excuse me. I forgot friends did stuff like this to friends. My mistake." His dark eyes flashed. "And what about Bruce? Are you just going to let Cherry dump him? That is the lowest!"

"It's not my fault. What happened was, Cherry—"

"Forget it. I don't even want to hear this. I gotta go."

Haley felt scared. Andy was mad, and all of her feelings were right at the surface where he could see them. She needed to hide. She needed Samantha Love. Taking a breath, she stepped into character. Her face changed, and the way she stood became tall and tight. Now she was ready. Now she could fight.

"Hey," she said, placing one hand on her hip, "Bruce is Cherry's problem, not yours and for sure not mine."

Andy looked startled. Haley felt a surge of confidence. Samantha Love always won an argument. She showered her opponent with buckets of words, until the victim almost drowned in them. Hit hard and fast. That's the Samantha Love way.

"And speaking of Bruce, I didn't like the way you ordered me around when he was here." In a nasal tone, she mimicked, " 'Haley, get Bruce this. Haley, get Bruce that.' Maybe you fetch for your parents, but don't expect me to do it for you and for sure don't ask me to do it for him. And another thing." She could hear her voice rise. "I didn't want to go to the dance with Bruce, but you went ahead and said yes!"

"I did ask you—"

"No, you said, 'That sounds like a great idea.' What was I supposed to say? No? Right in front of him? This whole thing is your fault, so back off!"

Now he seemed to blaze. Clenching his fists, he said, "MY fault! Listen, Haley—"

"You are not my boss," Haley cut in. "You can't make decisions for me!"

Andy leaped to his feet. His jacket had been draped over the back of the chair. With jerking motions, he pulled it on. "You know, Haley, you've get a real problem," he began.

"Not anymore. You're leaving."

"Is that supposed to hurt or something? Get a new writer." He glared at her. "The thing is, there's only one Bruce. Maybe he's weird, but at least he's always weird the same way. But you, you're two people. I see the way you act around me when you're with Cherry. It's like I'm not even there. You've been late every day just so no one will see you walking with me, right? I'm not stupid, Haley."

"You're not?" She narrowed her eyes and grabbed a line straight out of "Family Love." "Don't make a snap decision on that one."

Andy's face contorted into a grimace. He grabbed his backpack, crunching the straps together in one fist. "I don't care about my grade anymore. You can go to the Halloween dance by yourself. I won't be there. I feel a sickness coming on." With that, he stomped out the door.

His words stung her as if she'd been smacked with a fist. "Wait!" she shouted. "I don't care if you don't go. That's fine by me! You want to know why? Because everybody likes me! I've got more friends than I need! More friends than you!" Tears bit her eyes, but she forced them back. "I'm a star!"

But Andy was gone. She was yelling at an empty kitchen.

"Mom!" Haley cried. Anger, embarrassment, fear, hurt all rolled through her in an endless wave. "Mom!" she cried louder. "Come here! I need you!"

There was no answer.

"MOM!" A half sob burst from Haley. Her mother

would be outraged at the way Andy had treated her. She might even call Rita and demand an apology from Andy. No one talked to Haley that way. NO ONE!

"Wait a minute, honey, I'll be right down!"

Haley heard the pounding of her mother's footsteps on the stairs, and the click of high heels. She entered the room wearing a dove-gray jacket and matching silk skirt. Small silver studs dotted her ears, a white silk blouse scalloped her neck, and her hair had been braided and folded into a bow. From four feet away, Haley could smell Eternity perfume.

"Honey, are you okay?" Her mother rushed to Haley's side. "You look like you've been crying! What happened?"

"It's just so awful!" Haley exploded. "Andy yelled at me! He said I was two people, and he won't go to the dance with me. He's standing me up. ME! He is such a jerk! I hate him!"

"Don't say that! You shouldn't hate anybody. Slow down, Haley, I can't understand what you're saying. And don't cry on my jacket, sweetheart. It's silk. Let me get you a tissue."

"I want you to call Andy's mother and tell her that her son is a toad. I want you to tell her we're going to sue him for breach of contract." Sniffing, Haley looked more closely at her mother. It dawned on her how different she appeared. "Are you going someplace?"

"Umm-humm." Her mother glanced up at the clock. "I guess this is a terrible time to tell you, but I have to leave in about two minutes." Smoothing her hair with her hand, she said, "I wanted to talk to you about it earlier, but Andy was here. At any rate, I want to hear about this dance thing. Why did he break the date?"

Haley stepped back. "First tell me where you're going."

"Well." Her mother tried to smile. "I've got a job interview. Rita arranged it for me, and this is the only time everyone could get together." She hesitated, then went on, "I'm very excited about this, honey."

What was left of Haley's control dissolved. "How can you do this to me? You can't just leave me! You can't go!"

"Honey, it's just an interview. Now that you're in school, it's time I got out and did something with my life. I'm sorry the timing is so bad, but that's the way it is. I'll only be gone a little while."

Stomping her foot, Haley cried, "No. I don't want you to! I don't want you to leave me! You can't get a job!"

"I'm afraid this isn't your decision to make," her mother said, her voice low. "It's mine."

The ground felt as if it were slipping away from Haley, like sand in the tide. "I'm your job," she sobbed. "And what about Andy? Aren't you going to help me?"

Sighing, her mother crossed her arms. "I think it's time that you solve some of your own problems, Haley. You're a big girl. You need to work things out for yourself."

"But—" She couldn't finish.

"Oh, Haley, don't cry. Come on, now." Folding her daughter in her arms, her mother rested her cheek on Haley's head. "Of course you're the most important thing to me. You'll always be my first priority. But the truth is, we need the money. And beyond that, I want to do something for me."

"This is the worst day of my life!" Haley sobbed a great, heaving sob. "Nothing's the same! Why does everything have to change?"

"Because that's the way real life is." Her mother took a quick look at her watch. "I'm sorry, we'll have to finish this later. Rita's called a special meeting, and I simply can't be late. But we'll talk as soon as I get back. I promise, honey, we'll talk."

Four minutes after Andy had stormed through the door, Haley's mother rushed away.

Abandoned! Her eyes so blurry with tears she could hardly see, Haley stumbled up the stairs to her bedroom. "Rosie," she sobbed. "I'm all alone." She wrapped the stuffed gorilla's arms around her.

"There's no one left but you, Rosie. What am I going to do?" Even as her tears disappeared into Rosie's fur, Haley knew that her life had become as artificial as the stuffed animal she clung to. Her star really had turned to dust.

Spiderwebs stretched across the classroom wall. Plastic worms, two-inch spiders, and crawly bugs dangled from its filmy edges. It was too early to be allowed in the school, but Haley had sneaked in anyway. She needed to be alone. She needed to think. Lifting the lid of her desk, she removed Andy's invitation and turned it over and over in her hands. Outside, kid noises muffled through the windows.

Before her mother could wake her that morning, Haley had gotten up, dressed, and left. With every step on the frosty ground, she knew. She was no longer the center. Of anything. First Sheena had dumped her, then Andy, then her own mother. It was all the fault of her stupid body!

She'd bitten her lip almost raw. If she'd only stayed cute and small, she could have remained in Hollywood, where people loved her. Now, in this little town with ordinary kids, she'd become less than ordinary. Andy knew that. Haley had to make sure that no one else saw it. It had never been more important that she stay

Samantha. She couldn't afford to lose the only fans she had left.

"Hey, Haley, whatcha doing here so early?" Cherry appeared at the classroom doorway, right underneath the fake spiderweb. Flipping on the lights, Cherry said, "I was looking for you by the swings, but Grace said she saw you go in. You know Mrs. Walter won't let us into class early."

The legs of a caterpillar brushed the top of Cherry's head. Today she had pulled her long hair into a high ponytail and fastened it with a barrette shaped like a ghost. Mindy and Grace trailed in behind.

"I just felt like coming inside. So I did."

"You picked a good day to come in, 'cause there's a faculty meeting this morning, and Walter won't get to class till just before the bell." Cherry dropped into a seat beside Haley. Mindy and Grace did the same. They made a triangle of smiling faces around her.

Cherry pinched the tip of her ear. Her three earrings were all in the Halloween theme: a black cat, a green witch, and a broomstick that dangled to her shoulder. Leaning back in her seat, she let her eyes slide over Haley. "Haley, I LOVE your clothes! Are they from your show?"

Haley forced a smile. "Yeah, it's a designer outfit." She plucked at a thread from her sleeve and added, "But it's getting too small."

"The dragons on your shirt are so cool! Can I have it when you grow out of it?" Mindy asked. She popped a piece of bubblegum between her teeth.

"Sure."

"I think those pants are outrageous!" Grace said reverently. "Black leather! Can you believe it? I'm the same size as Mindy. Can I have those? I mean, some-day."

"Why not?"

"Oh, wow," Grace breathed. "Hurry and grow!"

Cherry crossed her legs and leaned closer to where Haley sat. "What's that in your hand?"

Haley's breathing stopped. She'd forgotten that she was holding Andy's invitation. "Nothing," she sputtered. "It's just a note—"

"Ohmygosh, is this it? Is this *the* invitation?" Cherry yanked the paper from Haley's fingertips. "It is! Oh, a poem from Andy Valdez. I wanted to see this thing!"

"No—wait!" Haley swung her hand into empty air.

"For sure this is going to be good." Opening the folded paper, Cherry read, " 'This is the chance, for a Halloween dance ...' " Smirking, she looked over at Mindy and Grace. "What did I tell you! I knew it would rhyme."

The girls snickered. Haley tried again to grab it, but Cherry pulled her hand away.

" 'That I promise you won't be the same,' " Cherry continued. " 'If you will just look ...' Ooohhh, this is sooo sweet."

"Knock it off, Cherry!"

" 'At the end of the hook ...' "

Haley jumped from her seat and thrust her hand right underneath Cherry's nose. "Give it! NOW!"

"Wait a second! What is your problem here? Are you in love or something?"

"No, I—"

"Then let me read it." As Cherry twisted away, her broomstick earrings whipped back and forth like windshield wipers on high.

Haley marched around the desk and planted herself in front of Cherry. "I'm not kidding. Give it back. NOW!"

Cherry stared hard. Haley stared back.

Just then, Bruce appeared at the doorway. His blond hair stood in little tufts from the wind, and his nose had turned a deep pink from the cold.

"Bruce, catch!" Cherry squealed. When she threw the invitation like a Frisbee, Bruce caught it with both hands. Cherry jumped up and ran over to where Bruce stood. "Great catch, Bruce! Now hand it over."

"Sure," Bruce said. "What is it?"

"It's just a note. It's from Mindy."

"No, it's not, Bruce!" Haley cried. She raced to where the two of them stood. "It's my invitation to the dance! I want it back!"

"Um, I um . . ." Bruce stammered.

"Don't give it to Cherry," Haley pleaded. "Give it to me."

"What is it with you, Haley?" Cherry turned on Haley, her voice like ice. "First you acted like you hated Andy, and now you're acting like you love him. Which is it?" Her eyes narrowed.

"Well, I—I'm an actress, so—"

"You call it acting, but I say it's lying. So, what's the deal? Were you a liar then, or are you a liar now?"

Other kids began showing up at the door. Chase and Tom stood shoulder to shoulder. Behind them came another cluster of girls. Everyone watched, curious to see what sort of drama was unfolding.

"Did you forget to take your medication this morning or what?" Haley asked, trying to smile. It was a line from "Family Love," but no one laughed.

"Give it a rest, Haley. We can hear you anytime we want, in reruns."

Haley was losing her balance. The mask had slipped, and everyone could see inside. With a supreme effort, she tried to call up Samantha Love one more time, but her back wouldn't straighten enough, her voice wouldn't sharpen. "I—I'm . . ."

"Um, Cherry, do you still want the note?"

"Forget it, Bruce." Eyes glittering, Cherry spat, "Give it to Haley. She's going to the dance with Andy, and they're both coming as losers. They won't even need costumes. They'll just show up and—"

But Cherry didn't get any further. Mrs. Walter had left a pail filled with plastic insects beside the door, ready to be used in the last of her Halloween decorations. In a move that was very un-Samantha like, Haley squatted down and reached into the Bucket O' Bugs.

Grabbing as many as she could, she tossed them, hard. "Why don't you just bug off, Cherry?" she cried.

The plastic insects pelted Cherry's head like black hail, sticking in her stiffly sprayed hair. Some of the boys at the door laughed. Bruce seemed to find his voice as he quipped, "Hey, Cherry, you're lookin' good. Spiders in your hair is a definite improvement."

"You think that's funny?" Cherry sputtered. Reaching down into the Bucket O' Bugs, she snatched a handful of plastic spiders and hurled them right into Bruce's chest. "There! Laugh at that!"

In a flash Haley picked up the bucket and dumped the entire contents onto Cherry's head.

"Bug fight!" Tom screamed.

After that Haley didn't know what happened. The kids that had been hanging by the door burst into the room and grabbed fistfuls of bugs off the floor. Someone yanked down a streamer, and soon black and orange balls of wadded-up crepe paper, bugs, and spiders whizzed across the room.

"You started this," Cherry shrieked at Haley.

"I guess I did!" Haley shouted back. She felt incredibly free. Free to do stupid things. Free to step off the line that she'd been walking ever since she'd become Samantha Love. Everyone but Cherry seemed to be caught up in the fun of the bug fight. Even Mindy and Grace were squealing.

"I hope you get suspended!" Cherry screamed. "I hope you and Valdez—"

"Oh, why don't you just shut up!" Haley howled. She grabbed Wilbur and smacked Cherry with him. Wilbur's head flew off and thumped across the floor, spilling straw as it rolled.

Cherry seized an eraser filled with chalk dust and hurled it at Haley. When it hit her on the face, yellow chalk dust powdered her eyebrows and lashes.

Safety! Haley needed protection. Diving behind Mrs. Walter's desk, she landed on top of Andy. "Where did you come from?" she yelled.

For an instant he just stared at her, and she at him. She could hear Cherry shouting, "They're behind the desk. Get them!" More plastic bugs and Wilbur stuffings flew over the teacher's desk to pelt them from above.

"Take some worms!" Andy commanded.

"What?"

He grabbed a container of Gummy Worms from Mrs. Walter's desk and shoved it underneath her nose. "Take some worms and throw them! Ready . . ." He grabbed a handful, then screamed, "FIRE!"

Leaping up from behind their fort, the two of them pelted the other kids with rainbow-colored Gummy Worms. Worms stuck to the walls, on shirts, and tangled in hair. Haley and Andy dropped back down to reload.

They sprang up again, and with a war cry, rained worms on their opponents. "Slime for the slimy!" Haley yelled.

"Down!" Andy ordered. "Reload."

A storm of plastic bugs hit them, but Andy didn't seem to notice as he kept up the barrage.

"You're good at this," Haley said.

"Thanks. You're not bad, either. Ready? Fire!"

It was suddenly quiet. With all of her strength, Haley screamed, "COWABUNGA!" as she flung a clump of worms over the desk. Leaping to her feet, she saw the worms land on Mrs. Walter, right in the center of her pumpkin-appliquéd sweater.

Frozen, Haley watched as one by one the worms dropped off Mrs. Walter's front and fell with tiny plunks onto the classroom floor. Haley sank down again behind the desk.

"HALEY AND ANDREW, GET UP THIS SECOND!" Mrs. Walter shouted.

Slowly, as if they were connected, Andy and Haley stood.

The room was a mess. Wilbur lay in pieces; the overturned trash can had spilled its insides; streamers dangled in limp clumps; and hoards of plastic bugs made the classroom look as if it had suffered a Biblical plague.

"I have never seen anything like this!" Mrs. Walter

cried. "Look at this mess! And to have it come from you, Andrew! You've always been a perfect student. This transformation is unbelievable. I simply don't know what to say."

As the starting bell rang, the rest of the kids slipped quietly into their seats, looking innocent. Their eyes were almost as big as Mrs. Walter's pumpkin appliqué.

"And you! Haley! I thought you were a star! The other children look up to you as an example! A star wouldn't behave this way. A star should have some self-control! A star should show other children how to act!"

"I'm not a star," Haley said softly.

"Excuse me?"

"I'm not a star. Not anymore. I'm just Haley Loring." She pulled a piece of crepe paper from her hair. "I can't show anybody else how to act, because ... because I'm just now learning how to act myself."

Some of the kids smirked, but for once, Haley didn't care. She no longer wanted to be Samantha Love. Even while she'd been throwing those worms, she'd realized that the kids might not like her anymore. And it didn't matter. Because if everyone loved Samantha—and Samantha wasn't real—that meant their friendships weren't real. There was nothing to save, so there was nothing to lose.

Storm clouds gathered overhead, and the air felt thick and heavy. Haley reached down to pick up a tree branch that had fallen onto the steps in front of her home. It was studded with knobs that looked like gnarled buttons. Peeling them off one by one, she tossed the scabs onto the cement. When the branch was bare she raised her eyes and looked up at the clouds.

"I think that cloud over there looks just like a witch," a voice from behind said.

Andy!

Whirling around, she saw him leaning against the trunk of a maple tree. He stared up at the sky, one hand shielding his eyes. "Nope, on second thought, it looks like a Cherry." With a wave he said, "Hi, Haley."

When she looked into his smile, her heart skipped a beat. Andy walked to the steps and dropped beside her.

"Are you in a lot of trouble?"

"Yeah," Haley answered. "My mom says I'm grounded. I've never been grounded in my life!"

"How long are you grounded for?"

Scraping the stick across the step, Haley grinned. "Just till tomorrow," she answered. "But it was only her first time, you know. How about you?"

"My mom says I have to stay in my room until I'm sixteen, and my dad says I have to stay there until I'm twenty-one. But I think they're only kidding. This was a shock for them. I've never been in trouble before."

They both leaned back on their elbows and looked up at the clouds. "About yesterday," he began. "I . . . I'm sorry. I kind of blew up, and I shouldn't have. My mom says I have a bad temper. I guess I kind of do."

"It's okay. A lot of what you said was right."

"A lot of what you said was right, too."

Punching his arm, she added, "This just means I won't have to worry about the pea pod thing."

Andy shook his head. "Nope. You're absolutely safe. No pollen shower from me."

She picked one last knob off the branch and squeezed it between her fingernails. "I'm sorry I said—"

"Yeah, well, let's just forget it. Okay?"

Letting out a breath, she said, "Okay."

"We've still got to work on our costumes, right?"

She looked at him. He was asking her to go to the dance with him. More than that, he was asking her if they could still be friends.

"It'll be Wilbur and Wilberta this Friday night," she declared.

"You got it!"

Haley wanted to tell him that, except for one evening as Wilberta the scarecrow, she intended to remain Haley Loring one hundred percent of the time, for the rest of her life. But she had the feeling Andy already knew.

"One more picture! I want one more picture! Please?"
Haley's mother cried. "You look so adorable."

"I'm too FAT!" Haley complained. "Andy stuffed
me so I'm as big as a house!"

"You made me just as big!" Andy retorted. "Look
at my legs! I can't even bend my knees!"

"I ain't nothin' but a hound dog," Bruce sang. With
the muttonchop sideburns and black leather coat, he
wasn't a half-bad Elvis. Haley had glued on the sideburns and sprayed inky washout dye in his hair. Andy
had loaned him an old Fisher-Price electric guitar. Since
Cherry had truly come down with a bad case of bronchi-
tis, Bruce was going to the Halloween dance without
her.

"Are you three ready?" her father asked.

"Ready," they chimed together.

"Then let's go!"

The cafeteria had been transformed into a shadowy
spook alley and other-worldly dance floor. Music blared

overhead, and in one corner of the room, ghosts, witches, robots, and mummies danced in time to the beat.

"Haley, Andrew, Bruce, come join the party. Isn't this fun?" Mrs. Walter bubbled as she greeted them at the door. She was dressed as a dinosaur. She wore lime-green material stuffed with cotton batting. Bright yellow triangles bristled down her back, and when she walked, her eighteen-inch dinosaur feet flopped against the floor. "The two of you look exactly like my old Wilbur did before his unfortunate demise," she told Haley and Andy.

"I'm so sorry about that, Mrs. Walter," Haley murmured.

"Well, you kids did a darn good cleanup job. Even if it took you all afternoon to do it. I'm counting on the fact that it will never happen again."

"Of course not!" Andy cried, just as Haley yelled, "No way!"

"Then let's forget it and enjoy the night." Swishing her tail, she turned to Bruce. "And this must be Elvis! I thought you were dead!"

"No, ma'am." Bruce sounded like he had a mouth full of marbles. "Ahh, those were just rumors." Strumming his guitar, Bruce crooned, "You're sorta good-lookin' but you ain't no friend of mine."

"I never knew he was such a ham," Andy whispered to Haley.

"Who would have guessed? That boy is a natural actor."

Bruce gyrated across the floor, singing as he went. He twisted past Grace and Vincent, who were dressed as Bonnie and Clyde.

115

"Hey, Bruce, you look great!" Grace called out.

"Thanks! Oh, let me be, your teddy bear."

Throwing back her head, Grace let out a bubbly laugh. She seemed to be having a wonderful time.

Harvest pumpkins filled every corner of the cafeteria. Punch and cookies had been spread out on an orange-and-black paper tablecloth. A mirrored ball spun slowly from the ceiling, casting snowflakes of light around the room.

Andy shifted from foot to foot. "Are you thirsty?" he asked Haley. "I'm dying of heat from this costume. Do you want some punch?"

"Sure!"

"Okay. I'll be right back." He waddled away toward the table. Haley watched as Mr. Sand, dressed as Roy Rogers, whipped a lasso through the air. It landed over the punch bowl.

"You and Andy look super, Haley. I'm glad you came." It was Mindy, surrounded by several girls from the class.

"Oh, thanks." Haley felt suddenly shy. Ever since the fight in Mrs. Walter's room, the girls had treated her as if she were invisible.

"Um, I know we haven't talked much since the *prob-lem!*" Mindy said, giving the word the Samantha Love inflection.

Haley didn't smile.

"So, anyway, we were wondering if you'd like to go trick-or-treating with us tomorrow night," Grace broke in.

The girls looked at her expectantly.

"I can't. I'm already going with Andy. But thanks a lot."

117

"Bring him along," Mindy said. "We can get some of the other guys and all go together. Chase'll round them up."

Grace cleared her throat. "You know, the Halloween flu idea really was lame. I am so glad I'm here. And I can't believe that Cherry got really truly sick. Incredible!"

Andy walked up, carrying two paper cups filled with punch. He eyed the girls suspiciously.

"They want us to go trick-or-treating with them tomorrow night. What do you think?" Haley asked him.

He shrugged, but carefully, so the punch wouldn't spill. "Did you tell them Bruce is with us?"

"Great," Grace said weakly, "Bruce can come, too. Does he have to bring the guitar?"

"He won't go without it."

"Well, then, meet at my house as soon as it gets dark."

Andy looked at Haley and asked, "Do you want to?"

"If you do."

He turned back to Grace and said, "Okay. We'll see you there."

At that moment, Sue Ann Johnson hurried over to the group. "Haley, is that you?" she asked. Sue Ann was dressed as a pioneer, with a purple gingham dress and white cotton bonnet. She looked almost exactly the same as she did every day in the office. Behind her, Sue Ann was pulling a second grade girl like a dog on a leash.

"Come on, don't be shy. She's nice!" Sue Ann whispered.

Crouching low, so that she could look the little girl

right in the eye, Haley said, "Hi, there. What's your name?"

"This is my niece, Jennifer Johnson. I brought her tonight just so she could meet you! She's such a big fan of yours! Even though you're not on it, we still watch the Love family every Thursday night!"

"Thank you," Haley said.

"Can I have your autograph?" Jennifer asked shyly. "I got some paper. I got a pen, too."

"Sure," Haley told her. "Let me just pull this glove off."

Jennifer stared at Haley with round eyes. When the little girl handed over the pen and paper, her hands shook.

"Samantha, you're my favorite person in the whole world," she said. "I like how you talk and stuff! Can you sign it that I'm your very best friend?"

"To my best friend, Jennifer," Haley wrote. She looked down at Jennifer, at her straight blond hair and clear eyes. Drawing a large heart, Haley wrote, "Love from the former Samantha Love, who is now the one, the only, the genuine ... HALEY LORING!"

Pointing to the "Samantha Love," Haley said, "This is who I pretended to be. But this ..." She pointed to the "Haley Loring." "This is who I really am."

Andy took her hand, and they headed for the dance floor.

Read All the Stories by
Beverly Cleary

☐ **HENRY HUGGINS**
70912-0 ($3.99 US/ $4.99 Can)

☐ **HENRY AND BEEZUS**
70914-7 ($3.99 US/ $4.99 Can)

☐ **HENRY AND THE CLUBHOUSE**
70915-5 ($3.99 US/ $4.99 Can)

☐ **ELLEN TEBBITS**
70913-9 ($3.99 US/ $4.99 Can)

☐ **HENRY AND RIBSY**
70917-1 ($3.99 US/ $4.99 Can)

☐ **BEEZUS AND RAMONA**
70918-X ($3.99 US/ $4.99 Can)

☐ **RAMONA AND HER FATHER**
70916-3 ($3.99 US/ $4.99 Can)

☐ **MITCH AND AMY**
70925-2 ($3.99 US/ $4.99 Can)

☐ **RUNAWAY RALPH**
70953-8 ($3.99 US/ $4.99 Can)

☐ **RAMONA QUIMBY, AGE 8**
70956-2 ($3.99 US/ $4.99 Can)

☐ **RIBSY**
70955-4 ($3.99 US/ $4.99 Can)

☐ **STRIDER**
71236-9 ($3.99 US/ $4.99 Can)

☐ **HENRY AND THE PAPER ROUTE**
70921-X ($3.99 US/ $4.99 Can)

☐ **RAMONA AND HER MOTHER**
70952-X ($3.99 US/ $4.99 Can)

☐ **OTIS SPOFFORD**
70919-8 ($3.99 US/ $4.99 Can)

☐ **THE MOUSE AND THE MOTORCYCLE**
70924-4 ($3.99 US/ $4.99 Can)

☐ **SOCKS**
70926-0 ($3.99 US/ $4.99 Can)

☐ **EMILY'S RUNAWAY IMAGINATION**
70923-6 ($3.99 US/ $4.99 Can)

☐ **MUGGIE MAGGIE**
71087-0 ($3.99 US/ $4.99 Can)

☐ **RAMONA THE PEST**
70954-6 ($3.99 US/ $4.99 Can)

☐ **RALPH S. MOUSE**
70957-0 ($3.99 US/ $4.99 Can)

☐ **DEAR MR. HENSHAW**
70958-9 ($3.99 US/ $4.99 Can)

☐ **RAMONA THE BRAVE**
70959-7 ($3.99 US/ $4.99 Can)

Coming Soon
☐ **RAMONA FOREVER**
70960-6 ($3.99 US/ $4.99 Can)